A Weapon of Mathematics

Other books by Charles Ott:

The Floor of the World
A Science Fiction Adventure

Something Made of Vacuum
A Science Fiction Romantic Comedy

A Weapon of Mathematics

Mathematics

by Charles Ott

Table of Contents

Zero

It's been said that when mathematicians discover a new series of numbers, the first thing they do is to give it an insulting name.

Negative numbers sound negative, but the Renaissance accountants could not keep books without them.

Irrational numbers are not irrational. They are just one more series of numbers, and a steam engine can't be designed without them.

Imaginary numbers are not imaginary: the laws that govern electronic circuits are based on them.

In the middle of the 21st century, a mathematician named John Timothy Offand at UCLA discovered a new series he called *commotic* numbers, after a Latin root meaning "deranged." Commotic numbers are, just like the other series, part of the laws of the physical world.

Offand did not fully understand, and could not control, what he had found. Civilization died in a wave of pain and force the survivors called the Sorcerer's Deluge. The Age of Magic had begun.

One

On a sunny early-autumn day, it was a fine thing to stroll the picturesque plaza of the old town of Dry Harbor. Hondoll, the King's Magician, wore his court-dandy clothes with swagger as he inspected the various booths around the perimeter. He was just twenty-two years old, curly haired, slim and elegant, with the studied presentation of one who had been promoted to the King's inner circle from low-class origins. His companion was Barrceil, a pretty blonde woman four years older and a little shorter than he was. He turned to her and said, "We have time for some shopping."

"The King sent me along to chaperon you," Barrceil said amiably. "I have to keep you on mission and keep you from calling attention to yourself. We're not here to shop."

"It's playing a role," Hondoll said. "Everybody comes here to buy. I'd be conspicuous if I didn't."

Barrceil followed with a carefully neutral expression while Hondoll dawdled past booths selling smoked fish, clothes, apples, pastries and wine, inspecting all with exaggerated aristocratic detachment. But when he came to a booth selling jewelry, all detachment vanished. Some of the jeweler's pieces were new, others old items scavenged from the debris of the Deluge.

Hondoll was as excited as a child when he held up a necklace for Barrceil to admire. It was costume jewelry, with a pendant showing a face in the shape of a crescent. "Look at this!" he said. "Eight hundred years old."

"That's nice," Barrceil said.

The fat man who owned the booth came up to say, "That's a theme we see every once in a while in old pieces, the face in that shape. I don't know what it signifies, if anything."

"It's the Moon," Hondoll said reverently. "How much for this?"

"Only six birds," the man said. "There's no gold or silver in it. But you're obviously a scholar, sir. What was the 'Moon'?"

"I'll take it," Hondoll said. Hondoll liked jewelry and was already wearing one gemmed earring and a ring on each hand. He opened his pouch and handed over six small coins with images of birds on them. He continued, "The Moon was a big rock in the sky. People used to think they saw a face in it. That's what this represents."

"How big?" the man asked.

"Big enough for people to walk on," Hondoll said, holding up the necklace to the sunlight. "In fact, some of the old books mention they built some kind of houses they could live in up there." A few people in the crowd looked at the necklace as he held it up, with oddly intent expressions.

"A rock big enough to live on, hanging in the sky without falling down," the jeweler said, smiling. "And they call *this* the Age of Magic. Enjoy your purchase, sir!"

Hondoll put the necklace into his pouch until he could clean up the ancient pewter, and resumed strolling the square. When he came to a booth selling "magic" artifacts – mirrors to create beauty, belts that granted strength in battle or protection against wounds, love potions and other catch-penny frauds – his expression darkened. A soldier was inspecting a rack of enchanted knives. Hondoll came up beside him and said, "Fellow, don't buy that. Magic doesn't work that way, and if it's for sale here, it's probably not even a well-tempered knife. There's an armorer across the square – if it were me, I'd buy there and get an honest weapon."

The old man behind the booth glared at him, and the soldier turned and looked down at Hondoll with no great friendliness. "You are an expert on knives, sir?" he asked.

"No, but I am a magician," Hondoll said. He spoke a brief spell and traced the diagram of its morphisms in the air with his fingers. A small flame danced in the air before him and followed his finger, until he extinguished it with a snap. "I can't say I know anything special about blades, but I do know there's no such thing as an enchanted dagger for sale in the public square. This fellow is just fooling you."

"I am licensed by the town council," the old man said. "You get away from my booth!"

"No, wait," the soldier said, turning back to

Hondoll. "One of my comrades had an enchanted dagger in a battle. He told me it flew like a bird, dragging his arm, and slew two men who were attacking him with swords."

"Your friend was a brave fighter, and skilled," Hondoll said. "But the bravery and skill were his, even though he believed in his enspelled knife. I actually can give those properties to a dagger, and it would make me a fearsome fighter even though I am not skilled at fighting and, I'm afraid, not very brave, either. But it would only work for *me*, because I understand the mathematics behind it. If I gave it to you, it would just be a knife. Magic *only* works for magicians, and only after long study. Take my advice, buy a better knife for less money from someone else."

The soldier looked uncertain. The old man came out from behind his table, ready to call the Civic Guard. Barrceil took Hondoll's arm and said to the other two, "Nice talking to you. We need to be on our way. Good day!" She dragged Hondoll away.

"Why do you show off like that?" she hissed, as they crossed the plaza. "We're here to sneak in, get what we came for and get out, remember? Besides, if that man had bought that dagger, it would have given him courage because he thought it was enchanted. Now even if he buys another dagger, he'll be full of doubts in a battle. You haven't done him a favor."

"The truth is always better than foolishness,"

5

Hondoll said lightly. "Let's get lunch." He spotted a tavern with a second-floor balcony overlooking the square, where a number of people were eating. "How about that?" he said, pointing up. "This town has a reputation for good fish dinners and we might catch a little breeze up there."

"I don't feel like climbing stairs," Barrceil said.

"We don't have to. I can see the balcony."

"Hondoll," Barrceil said in a low voice, "I know you can open a portal to that space and so could I. Don't you dare. You're conspicuous enough just walking around in court clothes. If you want to eat there, we'll both climb up the stairs. Now put your fingers down."

The first floor of the tavern was crowded with men and women at tables, eating food that smelled good. Hondoll looked sharply, standing in the doorway, then stepped back and tapped Barrceil on the shoulder. "Look in there," he said. "Only men on one side, only women on the other, with an aisle in the middle between them. When did that start happening? I've never seen that in the capital."

"I've heard of it," Barrceil said. "It's a small-town thing, at least so far. It's that Panhegan cult. They've decided men and women shouldn't eat together."

Hondoll snorted and said, "You know, I'm too young to start getting nostalgic about the good old days, but nobody had ever heard of these wet-brains five years ago and now they're bold enough to start telling people where they can sit. I'm not going to let fanatics push me around. Or you either, of course."

"Let's see what happens when we go in," Barrceil said reasonably. "I'm hungry."

The landlord was tending bar downstairs. When he saw them come in together, he waved up them up the wooden stairs to the second floor. They were met at the top of the stairs by a waiter who seated them together by the balcony railing, without comment. There were other tables with men and women dining together.

"Look at the tablecloths," Hondoll said sourly, when the waiter had left. "Green up here, black and gray downstairs. Cult colors. Apparently this floor is for the Carche cult, where men and women are allowed to sit together, and downstairs is for the Panhegan people, and you have to pick one side or the other to get lunch."

"I've got relatives in this town, so I come here once in a while," Barrceil said, "and it wasn't like this six months ago. Things are changing."

There was a little breeze to make them comfortable, and they had a fine view over the plaza. The waiter took their order for beer and meals of fish spiced and cooked in the local style.

Eight hundred years before, Dry Harbor had been the center of the Sorcerer's Deluge, a wave of force that had swept the entire world. The town had had a real harbor in those days, and a different name. When the Moon was whisked out of the sky, the tide receded from the harbor and never came back. The town still fished, but the new shoreline was almost a mile away.

Most of the buildings were made of old bricks salvaged from walls that had burst apart in the Deluge. Hondoll looked down idly. Two sides of the plaza were fronted with buildings holding taverns like the one they were in, offices, stables, and merchants.

The other two sides had temples facing each other. The temple of the Unborn God Panhegan was high and pretentious, made of bricks painted in gray with black cornices. It had stained glass windows and a broad stair leading up to doors that were three times the height of a man. The temple of the Unborn God Carche was lower and wider, painted in yellow and green, with a colonnaded porch.

The waiter brought glasses of beer and set them on the table. The beer was a little warm. Barrceil spoke a spell and traced the diagram with her fingers, and their beers became cold. The waiter happened to notice, and asked her, "Ma'am, are you a magician?" At her nod, he added artlessly, "You don't look like a wizard," and Barrceil rolled her eyes.

"Our town magician is late on his rounds and we're running out of ice," the waiter continued. "If you could help us out, I'm sure the landlord would be appreciative. Our ice-box is downstairs."

"Sure, I'll go," Barrceil said, and waved Hondoll down when he began to stand. "You sit, you sit. I'll take care of it." She followed the waiter back down the stairs.

Hondoll noticed a faint sound of music in the air. In fact, there were two sources of brassy music coming from two directions. The people on the plaza looked up.

Barrceil came back up after a minute, along with the waiter, who was carrying their food. "Lunch is paid for," she said with satisfaction as she sat down. "They had a lot of fish in the kitchen that could have spoiled until I froze up a couple of big tubs of ice for them. Also our drinks are free." The baked fish smelled delicious.

"Do you notice," Hondoll said, digging into his food, "that there are no *normal* churches on this town square?"

"There used to be," Barrceil said. "A few years ago there was a shrine of the Ocean Mother over there, and the Church of the Blessed Sun was next to it. I forget what was on that side before the Carche people took over."

"I was raised in the Church of the Blessed Sun," Hondoll mentioned.

"Me, too," Barrceil said. "Did you get caught up in the 'New Theology' thing?"

Hondoll smiled. "When I was a teenager, yes. They sent our church a new preacher fresh out of seminary, and he was all full of sermons

9

about how the Sun is a blessing from God, one of the symbols of God, but not God itself, and all the old folks ..."

"Ignored him and prayed directly to the Sun anyway," Barrceil finished, grinning. "My church, too."

Hondoll's expression went a little soft. "You know," he said, "we all used to stand outside on sunny days and sing hymns, and raise our faces to the Sun before meals, and ... I don't know. I stopped going to church once I got to university because it seemed sort of rustic, but now ..."

"Compared to these new crazies, it all seems pretty wholesome, doesn't it?" Barrceil said. "I stopped going too, and a lot of people did. Maybe that's what made room for these new cults."

"Do you hear that music?"

"They're parading with marching bands," Barrceil said. "Both cults, I think. They're heading this way." The music was loud enough to create a faint echo from the hills around the town.

"That's annoying," Hondoll said. "If they come here I'll quiet them down."

Barrceil gave him a sharp look. "You will *not*," she said. "This isn't our town, Hondoll. Let the local magicians, or the Civic Guard, quiet them down if they want to."

"If there's anything more annoying than superstitious fools, it's *loud* superstitious fools. But anyway, I developed a modification for that spell and I can quiet the noise just for us. They won't have to notice."

"You've been working on that equation?"

"I'm afraid I invented it," Hondoll said ruefully. "It's actually a variant of my spell for amplifying sound."

"*You* invented that damned amplifier spell?" Barrceil said. "That one started going around when I first got to university. For a couple of months I couldn't sleep because boys from the math department were having loud parties with music, trying to convince people they weren't bookworms or something. I would've strangled whoever wrote that spell if I had met him, until the counter-spell finally came out. But wait, you must have been ..."

"Twelve years old," Hondoll said, staring down at his plate. "I wrote those equations to try to impress the magician in my village so he would sponsor me for the gymnasium, and he passed them on to the college boys and they started using them just as soon as they had enough education to understand them. I'm sorry, I'm sorry. These days I never release anything I'm working on until I've thought about how it will be used, or misused. But I was a boy then."

"I've studied that spell. That was some elegant math, however annoying it was in practice. I should have realized it was you. You were – what? Fourteen? – when you entered the university?"

Hondoll nodded, and returned to his eating.

Down below, there was an anxious stir in the town square. Merchants were closing up their booths, folding their awnings and packing up their goods in rolling wagons. People began leaving the square, careful to collect their children and hustle them on ahead. The music grew even louder, and now they could hear the tramp of feet from the marching parades.

As Hondoll and Barrceil watched from their balcony, two columns of marching cultists entered the square from opposite sides. They both had marching bands playing cheerful loud music, and appeared in high good spirits. They waved flags and signs.

The Panhegan marchers wore gray and black, and their Unborn God was represented on their flags as a dragon. Men, women and children carried signs saying:

PANHEGAN. ONLY THE VIRTUOUS WILL LIVE PAST HIS MIGHTY BIRTH!

AWAIT HIS BIRTH WITH CAREFUL PREPARATION!

REPENT AND CHOOSE TO LIVE!

The Unborn God Carche was represented as a snake. His followers wore green and yellow and carried signs saying:

CARCHE. JOY IS FREELY OFFERED. WILL YOU TAKE IT?

LOVE WILL CONQUER THE UNLOVING.

The Panhegan cultists were stiff and censorious, holding their flags upright. The Carche cultists were mostly drunk and coarsely jolly. Each group waved its flags tauntingly at those on the other side of the square. The flagpoles were stout enough to use as cudgels.

The crowd of people who had been in the square had melted away. In the tavern, the diners around Hondoll and Barrceil stood and hurried to the exits. Some from the second floor dining room joined the Carche crowd, some from downstairs joined the Panhegan crowd, others made a hasty exit to side streets.

Hondoll sipped at his beer, then spoke a spell and traced its diagram with his fingers. The noise level subsided, although no one in the plaza seemed to notice. He returned to his lunch.

Barrceil watched, wide-eyed, as the two sides formed ranks. It was obvious that they were enjoying themselves, were looking forward to their encounter, and were ready to fight. Their flagpoles were were held ready to that use. Barrceil stood.

"Relax," Hondoll said to her. "All the bystanders are gone by now. The Civic Guard will be here in a few minutes, I'm sure. Let them beat each others' brains out if they want to. Obviously they do want to."

"There are children down there," Barrceil said tightly. "Let me see if I can't make them more loving." She began a spell of emotional manipulation, inducing a feeling of love into all of the people she could see from the balcony. She spoke the terms of the equation and traced the diagram of its morphisms, working with the quickness and precision of a university-trained magician.

Hondoll watched, still eating. "I wouldn't

use that," he said mildly. "It's not reliable on crowds."

Barrceil continued anyway. Across the plaza, no one looked up to notice her, but a ripple seemed to run through both crowds. The cultists turned to look at the others in their own group, and it became obvious her spell was affecting them. Their eyes met the eyes of their fellows, then turned back to their opponents. The music dwindled to a series of squawks and whistles, then died.

Each side launched into battle against the other. The two crowds raced toward each other and met in the middle of the plaza, swinging flag poles and signs, punching and screaming.

"I think your spell made them love their own side, which made them hate the other cult more," Hondoll said with infuriating calm.

Barrceil invoked another spell, with different coefficients than the first. "Calm," she said.

The cultists attacked each other with even more fury. "They want to be calm," Hondoll said, "but now they're convinced the other side is spoiling their calm mood, so they're even angrier. I don't recommend using emotional spells on more than about five or six people at once." He ate another bite of his fish while Barrceil looked down at the melee with wide eyes.

A rock thrown up from the crowd hit and bounced off their table.

Hondoll stood and glared down at the crowd. He invoked a spell with chanting and gestures, and translucent planes formed at the sides of the square, of immaterial zero thickness but yet impassable. Using another spell, he distributed his voice that each member of the crowd could hear him perfectly, even though he spoke in a normal tone.

"I am Hondoll, the King's Magician," he said. "I am charged with maintaining good order in the King's realm, and you are disturbing that order. Let me shine a light on your conduct."

He invoked another spell, with an exact nicety of speech and gesture. In the sunny sky above the square, a second sun appeared, framed in a rectangle of a slightly different blue sky. In the square, but only in the square, the light was doubled. "This extra light will show you the error of your actions," Hondoll said with dangerous smoothness.

After a moment, he used the spell again, and a third image of the sun shone down on the square. The light was blinding, bleaching away all colors. The people fell silent, cringing and pulling up their clothing to cover their faces. All fighting had stopped. "Hondoll ..." Barrceil said anxiously.

"Another," Hondoll said, still quietly. He invoked the same spell and a fourth sun appeared, forming an intolerable bright light. Cultists fell and cried, and many of their faces were red and blistered. Parents tried to shield their children with their bodies or with their flags.

"Hondoll, stop it! You'll kill them!" Barrceil cried. She began invoking her own spells, building opaque rectangles in the air to block the sunlight. "Stop it, stop it!"

With another gesture, Hondoll relaxed the barriers around the square, and those who could move fled in every direction with panicked cries. There were fallen bodies on the pavement, most of them still moving.

Hondoll allowed the other patches of sunny sky to wink out, and the natural sunlight returned. Barrceil relaxed her spells as well. A dozen officers of the Civic Guard had arrived, and they carried away all of the fallen cultists, glancing up with fearful eyes at Hondoll and Barrceil.

Their fish dinners had cooled off. Hondoll spoke a brief spell to warm both plates up, another to chill the beers again, and then resumed eating. He was smiling.

Two

The old harbor of Dry Harbor was now an expanse of sandy, salty mud, wet and smelly under the afternoon sun. Nothing grew on it but patches of tough sawgrass. It was so unstable that over the course of eight hundred years, no one had tried to build anything more ambitious than a wooden walkway from the old concrete quays down to the new shoreline a mile away. Old boats littered the ground, ragged from weather and looting. Hondoll and Barrceil sat on the gunwales of an old fiberglass sail boat. The hull was still sound, but was sunk into the mud.

Magic had made their job of excavating the hull easier but not less tedious. Each of them was studying a wide metal pan. For each of them, a small stream of clear water poured out of the air, washed the mud from the inside of the hull up in an unnatural arch so that it landed in the pan, then poured into a bucket which emptied itself every few minutes. They searched the pans for paper fragments or any debris that might be informative, and looked at the deepening holes in the mud to see what might be uncovered.

To shield them from the sun and hot, humid air, Hondoll had magicked a rectangle above them that presented a gray sky from some wintry place. Cold air settled down on them from this aperture. It was not really a comfortable compromise with the heat, but Hondoll was too intent to spend the time to arrange it better.

Barrceil was sensibly dressed for outdoor work in plain cotton clothes. Hondoll still wore his court finery, which was getting muddy.

"Look what I found," Barrceil said. She reached into the mud and extracted three cans of a six-pack of beer, still held together with the plastic retainer. "Eight hundred years old, and the aluminum is still solid and the plastic is just a little bit crackly. They sure knew how to build disposable stuff to last through the ages, back then." She held the cans into her stream of clean water to rinse them off.

"Offand's actual beer?" Hondoll said, his eyes wide. "Do you suppose we could still drink it? Just think of that!"

"Do you know a spell that would guarantee to make it healthy? Because I don't. I wouldn't touch it, myself."

"I suppose not," Hondoll said reluctantly. "Now that you mention it, though, I need a beer." Magic could connect the place where he was with any other place he could visualize clearly enough. He was a regular at a tavern called *The Goose*, back in the capital city ten miles away, and could easily visualize a particular spot at the bar. He spoke the magical expression aloud and traced the diagram of its morphisms in the air with his fingers. A wavering circle with a view of the back of the bar opened in the air in front of him. He called for the bartender, who walked into the field of view. Hondoll passed three coins across, and accepted cold glasses of beer for himself and Barrceil. With a word of thanks, he closed the connection by a hand gesture. *The Goose* was near the university and a favorite of students in the department of mathematics. The bartenders were quite used to sudden apparitions in the air. Hondoll was unusual only in that, unlike students, he could afford to add a tip.

They stopped the streams of water and sat on the gunwale, drinking their beers. "What if this really was Offand's boat," Barrceil said, "and we really do find some old notes of his? He triggered the Deluge because he didn't know enough to control his magic. Could we bring a new deluge just by reading his notes?"

Hondoll was silent for a long moment. "I don't think so," he said finally. "We understand that math now in ways that Offand didn't. All I can promise to do is be careful if we actually find something. But Barrceil, I really can't walk away from this. You know me well enough to know that."

"I suppose. Me neither, when it boils right down."

"That's why I was willing to let you come with me for this. If we do find anything, I only want people I can trust to know about it. You have the skill to understand it without causing harm. I wouldn't trust even most degreed magicians for that, much less the public."

"Also you had to let me come with you,"

Barrceil said peaceably. "The King figured you'd call attention to yourself on this trip, which is exactly what you did. Look over at the quays, there. Those two loafers weren't there when we started. Sure looks to me like they're watching us."

Hondoll looked at the two men lounging on the concrete walkway that had marked the old waterline, and said nothing. He and Barrceil finished their beers, and Hondoll conscientiously re-opened the portal and returned the glasses to the tavern before returning to his search.

They dug deeper and deeper into the old boat. They found the remains of a life jacket, the plastic foam inserts still intact although the cloth had long since rotted away. They found some apricot pits, apparently from a snack the boat's owner had prepared. They found the remains of a boat hook, the wooden handle worm-eaten and the metal corroded almost to nothing.

"How did you find out this boat belonged to Offand?" Barrceil asked, her eyes on her pan.

"Poking around the university library," Hondoll said, keeping his own eyes down. "I got interested in some work Goodlow – you've heard of him? – did back in Offand's day. Goodlow had a mathematician friend who was nobody special, but the library happened to have a letter from that guy to Goodlow. I don't think anybody ever bothered to read it before. The guy mentioned visiting Offand on his boat in this harbor, and said that Offand liked to come out here just to have a quiet place to work. We know Offand preferred to work with pencil and paper rather than on a computer or something. So if this is the right boat, and if Offand worked here and if he kept a notebook on the boat and if he stored that notebook someplace where it might have survived ... why, then I'll be the only one to read it since the Deluge."

"Is this where he triggered the Deluge?"

"Tradition says he was at his desk at home when that happened."

"So why are you chasing a dumb chance like that?"

"I don't know. I just have this feeling, a very strong feeling, that there's something here. You ever get hunches like that?"

"No," Barrceil said, looking at him, then said, "Hey! Look at this." Her stream of water had uncovered the corner of a gray plastic box. She scooped away mud with her hands and prized it up. It was a waterproof hinged case with a handle, not very large, with a corroded key lock. Hondoll immediately reached for it and she let him take it. He tipped the case, and something thumped within it. "It's still sealed," he said wonderingly. "There's air inside, not water, not mud."

He spoke a spell, looking intently at the lock while tracing the graph with his fingers, and the lock vanished from the box and reappeared in the air a foot away, falling to the mud with a small sound. He pulled the box open. The rim of the box was sealed with a soft plastic gasket that had successfully kept out water for eight hundred years.

The box held a battery-dead calculator, a few pencils, a brown eraser that had hardened and cracked, and a hand-written notebook with a tan paper cover. Hondoll and Barrceil looked at each other. Hondoll picked up the notebook and opened it reverently. "Offand," he said, barely breathing. "Offand's notes."

"Hondoll," Barrceil said in a low voice, "we need to get out of here."

Hondoll looked up to see that the crowd on the quays had increased to a dozen men. They were dressed in ordinary work clothes, but the leader group wore a distinctive hat he knew was the sign of a priest of Carche. The men jumped down from the old quay and advanced on Offand's boat.

Hondoll quickly erected a translucent barrier in a circle around them, saying "They're probably just trying to rob us – I guess I shouldn't have worn expensive clothes. I don't want to get run out – there might be more treasures on this boat. They can't get through that barrier, but ..." He stopped in confusion, then said, "I don't know, something feels bad here. Barrceil, you set up a barrier inside this one. I know, it shouldn't be necessary. But do it anyway."

Barrceil glanced at him but erected her own magical cylinder. Seen through two translucent layers, the men were vague shapes milling around them.

Hondoll pulled a notebook out of his tunic and put it in the plastic box. He glanced down at Offand's notebook, worked a brief spell and tucked the notebook into his tunic. They watched, wide-eyed, as the men bumped and rammed against the immovable barrier.

"All right, I'm nervous," Hondoll said. "Let's get out of here." He began invoking another portal, joined to the same tavern he had already contacted to avoid having to visualize someplace else.

He did not complete it. He and Barrceil watched, open-mouthed, as the priest of Carche touched their barriers and opened holes in them as though glass had melted. The priest stepped in, stepped up to Barrceil and punched her accurately in the jaw, knocking her out. Hondoll was next.

When Hondoll fell unconscious, his barrier, his overhead portal to cooler weather and the streams of water winked out of existence.

Three

Hondoll returned to awareness in a quiet room, facing a fat man in expensive, stylized robes of green and yellow in front of him. "I am Wal Osrey Bonder, a priest of the Unborn God Carche. You are a guest in a house in the country where no one will think to look for you," the man said, as soon as Hondoll's eyes were open. "We have given significant thought as to how to secure a wizard of your strength, and we have finally decided that simpler is better. Of course you are bound to your chair and your hands fettered, but please observe the three bowmen facing you. Their bows are strong and hard to pull, so at any moment only one will have his bow drawn and an arrow aimed at you. However, each of them is capable of drawing and shooting in a moment. So here is your situation: if you attempt to speak a spell, you will be shot through the heart by an archer before the third syllable. If you succeed in speaking a spell which disables the archers, the one with a cocked bow will be stricken and will release the string, which will also shoot you dead. We have put you in this position, which we regret, so that we can talk to you and persuade you of the virtue of our cause. Is there anything we can provide for you?"

"Water," Hondoll said thickly. The light of sunset poured in through the open windows of the room, a pleasant but impersonal bedroom that might have been intended for guests. A garden was visible outside. Curtains fluttered in the breeze, and Bonder was leaning casually on a wooden dresser.

Hondoll's arms were fixed to the chair arms by immovable metal bands. A servant, careful not to get between the archers and Hondoll, extended a cup of water at the end of a stick to Hondoll's mouth, and Hondoll drank with a certain amount of spillage. "Where is Barrceil?" he asked.

"She is safe, but she is not here. We mean no harm to either of you, Hondoll."

"I am the King's Magician. The King's men will find me," Hondoll said.

"We think not," Bonder replied politely. "First, our patron, whose house this is, is not known to be an adherent of Carche and is of such high rank that the King, even if he should suspect this, will hesitate to impugn him. You are in a room which has a pleasant view over the garden but is not visible from the outside, and we have our own magicians to obscure your presence in various ways. Our magicians are not your equal, of course, because no one is, but we have many of them who are devoted to the god Carche. I believe that you yourself attended some of our mysteries when you were in university, didn't you?"

Hondoll gave a rueful smile. "At that age, a young man does many things for love. I was in love with someone who was a devotee of Carche.

But orgies and drunkenness never appealed to me."

"A young man named Rendenen, wasn't it? You see, we know much about you, Master Magician," Bonder said. He pulled a chair to him and sat companionably, facing Hondoll. "But Hondoll, Carche is not a vulgar god of orgies and drunkenness. He is a god of love, of joy, of the celebration of the world. Those who worship him are exalted and led to a higher state of mind. This is the virtue we want to bring you to experience."

"I loved Rendenen," Hondoll said, "and he said he loved me, and then he dragged me to your 'mysteries', which invariably ended in drinking, fornication, lewdness and at the end, vomiting and face-down black-outs. I am not attracted by worship like that."

"Students at the university are often intemperate in their appetites, aren't they? I studied there myself, fifteen years or so before you attended. But you must understand that those who love Carche cannot sin while exalted in his presence. All things become holy and spiritual, all things are permitted to us – this is why we love a god who raises us, who sanctifies our freedom and opens possibilities for us. Hondoll, you can be more than you are, more than you ever hoped you could be! Carche can lead you to open the doors of your soul, to reveal mysteries you did not know you had in you."

"Why should I talk to you, you besotted fool?"

Bonder did not take offense. "Why, for the obvious reason that I will kill you if you don't. I do not want you opposing us as we sweep to victory over the sour Panhegan, and claim the temporal power that Carche ought to wield. How much better it would be, for you, for the benefit of your soul and for our nation, if you joined up and used your magic on our behalf. Hondoll, I have not begun to enumerate all the blessings that joining Carche can bring you. In contrast, your death is worth nothing, not to me and certainly not to you."

"Bring in one of your wizards," Hondoll said. "I need some magical assistance, and I don't want to alarm you by attempting a spell."

Bonder gestured to a guard, who called out in the hallway. In a moment a skinny, shy young man entered. Hondoll regarded him.

"Hello, Nanquan," Hondoll said. "Did you finally graduate? The last time I saw you, I was tutoring you through your class in – what was it, analytic geometry?"

"I did graduate," Nanquan said, abashed.

"Can you help me out here? My bowels are full and I can't relieve myself while I am confined to this chair. No, wait. Tell me what you're going to do before you speak the spell. Forgive me if I show a lack of confidence, but I want to be sure you're using the right tools before you do an extraction from the inside of my body."

They had a few moments of technical

conversation. Finally, Hondoll said, "All right. Do that, please. I am uncomfortable." Nanquan invoked a spell, using university-trained diction and gestures. There was a wet plopping sound from outside the window. "Thank you. I think you hit the garden," Hondoll said wryly. "That will stink for a while, but it will be good fertilizer for my lord Kablevon's flowers. I feel better now."

"You are trying to impress me," Bonder said, "but this is not Kablevon's house that you are in."

"Bonder, I have been a guest in this house when Kablevon hosted the King. You don't know as much about me as you imagine. Now that I think about it, Kablevon hinted at some unusual sexual tastes, so I suppose that's what you offered him for his support. Nanquan, didn't you bring your girlfriend to one tutoring session I had with you? She seemed like a nice enough girl and she liked you. You can attract wholesome love. What need have you of Carche?"

"You don't understand," Nanquan said, with a glance at Bonder. "Carche inspires wholesome love, which is why he is lovable and all must love him."

"Nanquan, leave us, and thank you," Bonder said. The windows were growing dark, and some of Bonder's men lit candles. When Nanquan had closed the door behind him, Bonder continued, "Hondoll, I won't have you trying to subvert my associates. Please understand that you will leave this room in the service of Carche or you will leave it not at all, and also understand that I honor and respect you and I am trying very hard to save your life, because Carche is a god of abundant life."

"Bonder, besides all the math, I did take a few other courses at university, including some history. The cult of Carche is not ancient. It began, what? Sixty years ago? Carche is not a god, Carche is an excuse for you to have a good time. A good time for those with strong stomachs, at least."

Bonder looked at him sharply. "Hondoll, you are a genius of mathematics and the premier magician of our age, aren't you?"

"In all modesty, I am," Hondoll said.

"Your power is stronger than any other magician I know, probably more than any other in the Kingdom."

"I think so."

"And yet you are confined here."

Hondoll looked pensive. "That's a good point," he said after a pause. "You should not be able to do this. How did you compel me here?"

"As a priest, I wield a portion – a tiny bit, really – of the power of the Unborn God Carche," Bonder said. "Carche's power is superior to magic, as you have discovered."

"You have spoken to this god?"

"No one speaks to him or is spoken to by him directly. He will speak to us when he is born. At present, he makes his power known to us by an inner light, by a conviction of spirit, by the peace that flows from following his will."

Hondoll made a rude noise. "I admit you've got something. You don't have a god."

"Suit yourself, for the moment," Bonder said mildly. "The god Carche will make himself known to you when it suits him, and to everyone when at last he is born. But you are right that we have power. Power to dominate, power to win. We can win – we will win – without your help. But with your help, the false cult of Panhegan could be destroyed and the rule of Carche established with much less loss of life. Think of the warm, living, valuable men and women who will be killed, who will leave grieving families and spouses and parents, in the battle to come. Now think how you can reduce that agony. You can be a hero, a protector, a savior of the people, Hondoll. Our victory is inevitable, but the agony of war is not. You can alleviate that agony, if you will."

"What happens to the followers of Panhegan?"

"They will be brought to joy, lovingly but irresistibly. Now I need to ask you, where is the notebook?"

Hondoll said, "I can't reach it with my hands bound. It's in an inside pocket of my tunic."

At a gesture from Bonder, one of the guards, standing carefully to one side, felt inside Hondoll's clothes and extracted the notebook

Hondoll was never without. It was small and had a black leather cover. The guard presented it to Bonder and stepped back.

"That's of no use to you," Hondoll said. "When I've got something ready to present, I always publish it. I have no secrets."

Bonder glanced at the book and put it aside. "Not your notebook," he said dangerously. "The Offand notebook. Where is it?"

"People have been looking for anything Offand did since the Deluge," Hondoll said.

"You had that notebook when you were in the boat. Where is it? I am under orders from the highest authority to use any means I need to to get it," Bonder said. "Please don't test me on this."

A ray of blackness crossed the ceiling, like the inverse of a beam of sunlight. The others did not see it, and Hondoll carefully averted his eyes once he noticed it. Bonder continued to speak, while further straight lines of blackness shot across the room, at various angles but all in a single plane. The archers saw them and called out to Bonder, who looked up in alarm. He hesitated, then tried to dodge out of the way as the rays merged.

The rays flowed together to form a black plane through Bonder's body, and he was cut in two pieces and died.

Hondoll was alone in the small part of the room delimited by the black surface, the air close and full of the smell of Bonder's blood. The window shattered, and a young man with a shaven head slid through feet first and landed on his feet with a flourish.

"Rendenen!" Hondoll cried.

"The very same," Rendenen said. "I was searching to rescue you anyway, and once that fool spoke my name I was able to zero in on his location." At his gesture, other planes formed from crossing black lines and broke the brick wall, which fell outward to expose the garden. Rendenen spoke a spell and gestured, and the bonds fell away from Hondoll so that he was free. Hondoll bent down and retrieved his notebook.

"Quickly, now," Rendenen said. "I can hold them off and I've got a carriage with your friends outside to take you into town, but I'm under attack here, as you can appreciate."

"How were you able to break the restraints?" Hondoll asked.

Rendenen looked at him and grinned with the smile Hondoll had loved a few years before. "Follow me out, now," he said. "We'll talk later. I can do this because I am fortified by the power of the god Panhegan."

"Can you find Barrceil?"

Rendenen looked startled. "I remember her. Did they capture her, too?" At Hondoll's look he continued, "I'm sorry, I don't have any information about her. I'll try to find her but we need to get you out of here first."

The sky was almost dark. They ran through

the garden. There was a two-horse carriage in the driveway with three of his colleagues, magicians in service to the King. They were ready with powerful protections for him. Hondoll climbed into the carriage. When he turned back, Rendenen was nowhere to be seen.

At a snap of the reins, the horses turned and dashed toward the city.

Four

Barrceil awoke feeling good, from a pleasant, vivid dream of romance. She was instantly suspicious. Spells to force certain emotional states on others were strongly restricted by the ethics code of the Collegium. One such spell induced amorous feelings, and every girl in the mathematics department at the university quickly learned to guard herself against it. Barrceil tested her own mind, concluded she had been the target of such a spell while she was knocked out, and was furious.

She was lying on a pad of tarpaulins in the bilge of a small wooden fishing boat. The boat stank of fish offal but the tarps seemed to be clean. An ocean breeze blew across her face. She opened her eyes cautiously and saw a stocky, gray-haired man with a weather-beaten face, sitting at the stern of the boat with his hand on the tiller. He wore an oilskin jacket and canvas trousers.

He saw her eyes open and said immediately, "You are safe, my lady. You have not been molested. I think you've detected the spell that was worked on you, but be serene: the magician who did it is not here any more."

"Where did he go?" Barrceil asked.

"I hit him in the head with an oar and pitched him overboard. I watched him drown. He was not able to recover himself enough to escape with magic and could not swim," the man said flatly.

Barrceil sat up and regarded him bitterly. "So somebody knocked me out at the beach, captured me, set me up for rape – but it's all this other guy's fault and you threw him overboard. You're a big hero, you saved me from a terrible fate and I should be grateful to you," she said. "I'm not giving you that. What's actually going on here?"

"Ma'am, my name is Fanward," the man said. "I did do that to protect you, because I could see what he intended. But I intended to drown him anyway. He worked his bad magic on my daughter while I was at sea some months ago. He didn't know that I knew, but I intended to kill him at the first opportunity."

"You're a cultist, right? Which damned god are you taking me to?"

"I was a follower of Carche, ma'am," Fanward said. "My family still follows that faith, but I do not. I was supposed to take you to the Great Mother but I'm taking you home instead. You live in the city of River's Lover, I think?"

"Yes, I do. What are you going to do?"

"I can't go home to Dry Harbor now. And I don't want to. My wife and my children have given themselves over to Carche so passionately that I don't feel like I even know them any more. I've betrayed Carche, and I don't doubt they'd turn me over to the Great Mother in an instant if I tried to go back."

Barrceil stood. The boat moved smoothly, without rocking. In fact, the sail was furled. Barrceil looked over the gunwale and concluded they were sailing by magic a few feet over the water. She looked sharply at Fanward. "The magician you killed ..."

"His name was Erstone, ma'am."

"Erstone. If he's dead, why is this boat still sailing by magic?"

"I control it myself. I am an amateur magician."

"And you're dressed up like a fisherman."

"No, ma'am. I really am a fisherman and this really is my boat. The priests told me to follow Erstone's orders. After I killed him, I enspelled the boat again and continued in a different direction." He smiled shyly. "Since I'm used to steering with the tiller, that's how I control the movement. Erstone just waved his hands in the air."

There was no hiding place on the boat for another person. Barrceil sat down again and said, "Talk to me. Tell me everything."

"It's simple enough. I was good at arithmetic in school," Fanward said, "but I could only stay until the fifth year, then I had to go help my father fishing. My teacher was good enough to give me some mathematics books and my father let me study at night, as long as nobody else knew I was doing it. We followed the Church of the Blessed Sun – before everybody in town went crazy for one or the other of the Unborn Gods, I mean – and the priest was able to get books for me from the city. I could go to the town library. After a while I was able to progress to the study of magic. I know a few things, not as much as a real magician, of course."

"Your education shows in your speech."

"Thank you. It's a blessing not to have to guard myself when I talk to you. I've had to hide all my life."

"If you know enough magic to lift and propel a boat like this," Barrceil asked, "why do you have to hide? Why are you still a fisherman?"

"To make a living and feed my family, ma'am," Fanward said. "In the capital city, I don't think you know how people out here think about magicians. If they knew I could do spells, I'd get blamed for everything – milk cows drying up, anybody's child getting sick, bad weather, bad harvest, bad fish – everything. In truth, my neighbors would have killed me, or my family, by now."

Barrceil hesitated a moment, then said, "I've met that attitude a few times, but you're right, it's different in River's Lover. Have you studied the defensive spells, to protect yourself?"

The sun was going down, the western sky aflame. Their shadows appeared to scamper up and down on the waves to the east of the boat. "I don't know those expressions, ma'am. Never got those books. When I try to write my own spells, it doesn't usually work well."

"Maybe I can teach you, later," Barrceil said. "Of course, I have protections I keep erected, but they didn't seem to help me very much. They just knocked me out and threw me in here."

"That's the influence of Carche," Fanward said. "His priests can weaken or dissolve any magic they don't like."

"How does that work?"

"I don't know, ma'am."

"Won't the other priests find you and cancel the magic you're using to drive this boat?"

"The influence his priests can wield only applies to magic they can see, at least until the god is born," Fanward said. "We're far enough away to be free of Carche's influence here, or so I hope."

"Do you know what the limits to this so-called god are?"

"No, ma'am."

"Do you know what happened to the man I was with, Hondoll?"

"No, ma'am."

Barrceil attempted to communicate with Hondoll, but could not establish a connection. She sat silently as the sun set and Venus appeared as the evening star. She looked up into the darkening sky, then looked at Fanward. "There is a spell, similar to the one that villain used on me, to compel an emotional commitment to honesty. I can't ethically use it on you without your permission. May I invoke that spell on you?"

"I give you permission," Fanward said formally.

Barrceil spoke the spell and traced the diagram of its morphisms with her finger. There was no visible effect, but she asked Fanward, "Are you now a follower of either Carche or Panhegan?"

"No, ma'am."

"You hate Carche? You will help me?" Fanward agreed to both questions. But Barrceil looked uncertain. "If Carche can nullify magic, how would I know if you're speaking truthfully?"

"I can say that I have always been a truthful man, except for concealing my reading and study," Fanward said. "I do say that. But of course, I have no way to convince you that I am not compelled by Carche, except to tell you that I know I am not."

Barrceil sighed. Fanward said, "Will you release me from the honesty spell now? It can lead to social awkwardness." She laughed, then took down her spell.

"The city is full of followers of both cults," Barrceil mused. "They stage these big parades and rallies and then fight with each other in the streets. I'm sure the Carche bunch will be told to look for you. Are you willing to risk coming with me?"

"My daughter is about your age, Doctor Barrceil. The cult of Carche used her badly and then turned her heart against anyone who refuses to worship him. That would be me, now. I hate Carche to just the same extent that I love my daughter."

"Call me Barrceil," she said quietly. "Hondoll is a member of the King's court, I'm his friend and I stand high enough in the Collegium to sponsor you for membership as a self-taught amateur. So you'll have upper-class rank too."

"Barrceil," Fanward said, and smiled.

She became brisk. "I see some lights up ahead. That's the city, right? Take down your magic and we'll enter the harbor as an ordinary fishing boat. I don't want to transfer to my home or any place in town without scouting around first."

Fanward spoke an expression with coefficients of opposite sign to the spell which put the boat in the air, and traced the runes with his fingers. The boat slowed to a stop and settled into the water. The evening was calm, with a light breeze, and the boat rocked gently.

Fanward stood and loosened lines to hoist the sail, then adjusted the sheets that held the boom steady. In a few moments he was able to resume his place at the tiller and guide them toward River's Lover.

He was a skillful sailor. They entered the harbor and, propelled by a light breeze, threaded a way between full-rigged ships. Barrceil crouched down, her head barely visible, and prepared weapon spells to defend them if attacked. But Fanward was able to call out to the harbormaster's clerk and get a berth without trouble. He tied up his boat, re-furled the sail, then jumped up on the dock and helped Barrceil climb out.

She provided the coins they had to pay for the berth, and they walked together up from the harbor into the city.

Barrceil dipped into her purse again to hire a hackney cab to take them, not directly to her home, but to an intersection nearby, from which she could reconnoiter.

The horse's hooves clacked loudly on the cobblestone pavement. A city lamplighter was just igniting the streetlights as they passed. Abruptly, Hondoll's voice spoke from the air to Barrceil, so low that neither Fanward nor the driver could hear it.

"Barrceil, this is Hondoll. Are you all right?"

"I am," she whispered. "You?"

"I've been rescued – I just got free. Can you get to the palace? The King wants to see us."

"I'll be there in a few minutes."

She spoke up and directed the driver to take them instead to the palace in the center of the city. The driver looked back with a glance at Barrceil's rumpled clothes and Fanward's fisherman's garb, but turned into a different street without comment.

Barrceil looked left and right, tensely on

guard, ready with spells of violence.

Five

Leovar, King of Juffland, entered the conference room with his leading general Benjaric. Both wore field clothes and carried swords. Hondoll stood immediately, still wearing his mud-stained court clothes. The King went to him and embraced him, then held him at arm's length. "I'm glad you're unharmed, but you look hard-used, man," the King commented. He turned to an aide standing behind the general and said, "Tell the cooks to bring up some food and beer." The aide left just as Barrceil and Fanward were brought in by an escort of three armed soldiers. After a quick consultation with the general, the soldiers took a station outside the door.

Barrceil exchanged a smile with Hondoll, then turned to the King and said, "Your Majesty." She began a curtsy.

The King waved her up. "We will be in military protocol for this meeting. Address me as 'sir' but no other respects are necessary. Doctor Barrceil, who is your companion?"

Fanward was visibly awestruck in the presence of the King. He tried to speak, then stopped to bow, tried to speak again and could not. "Sir, this is Fanward," Barrceil said, coming to his rescue. "He is a fisherman and amateur magician, and he rescued me from capture by the cult of Carche. He is a fugitive from Carche and can tell us about them."

"Welcome, Goodman Fanward," the King said. "Everyone, please be seated around the table. Ah, here comes food." Stewards arrived with a steaming pot of vegetable soup and mugs of beer. "We'll take a moment to eat and compose ourselves." The stewards ladled out a bowl for the King, then served the others. General Benjaric declined soup with a gesture, and Fanward just shook his head, wide-eyed.

The King smiled and said quietly, "Fanward, take some soup." Fanward accepted his soup and spooned it up with painstaking attention. The King ate a little, then waited for Hondoll and Barrceil to finish.

Leovar was a rangy, vigorous man in his late thirties. He had deep-set eyes and big ears, and his only mark of rank was a gold circlet on his short brown hair. He turned and had a soft-voiced conversation with his general, too low for Hondoll to hear.

Presently Hondoll put down his soup, drank some beer and sat up straight. Barrceil finished also, and Fanward pushed his soup away. "Hondoll," the King said, "You've told me something of your story remotely, but tell it again in person for everyone. Barrceil, then you."

Hondoll related his story. When he reached the part about being confined in Lord Kablevon's house, the King stopped him. He turned to Benjaric. "General," he said, "it is intolerable to have my ministers kidnapped. Have Kablevon brought in. He will find that his rank is not as much of a protection as he thought. Go in force, and bring some of your magicians along with the arresting party. Anyone you find in his house, have them detained as well." Benjaric nodded and went out to talk to an aide. When he returned, the King gestured for Hondoll to continue.

When Hondoll had finished his story, Barrceil broke in anxiously, "Did they get the Offand notebook?"

"No," Hondoll said, pulling a black leather notebook out of his tunic pocket. "I've still got it."

"That's your notebook," she said.

"The best disguise," Hondoll said, grinning, "is the least. I disguised this notebook as a notebook." He spoke the same spell he had used on the beach, but with negative coefficients, and the black leather faded away to tan paper. "That Bonder who was threatening me, he was a real fool. He never noticed this. If Rendenen hadn't killed him, I think the other Carche priests would have."

General Benjaric looked at the book in wonder. "Offand's own notebook?" he asked. "I can't imagine the power that artifact must have. Is it safe to handle?"

"General, forgive me for correcting you, but it doesn't work that way," Hondoll said. "All those 'magic' beans and whatnot they sell in the city square, that's all fraud. There's no such thing as a magic object. Magic needs a magician, and never works outside of his or her presence." He turned to the King, held up the notebook and said, "Thank you for letting me go and find this. I want to sit down and read through it, but you shouldn't expect anything dramatic. I'm sure I will be interested, but there might not be anything of importance to anybody else. That reminds me, I need to get my own notebook back. Will you excuse me a moment?" Using the same spell he had used for obtaining beer, Hondoll opened a portal to the sunken hull of Offand's boat, reached through it to retrieve the gray plastic box, then relaxed the portal. If anyone was still there, they apparently did not notice his hands reaching out of the air.

Hondoll opened the box, extracted his notebook and remarked, "Whoa. All kinds of 'magical' artifacts here. Offand's dead calculator, Offand's dried-up pencil eraser and Offand's original pencils, which are probably still good. Anybody need a pencil?"

"If the calculator batteries aren't all nasty, couldn't you restore them?" Barrceil asked.

"*I* couldn't, myself," Hondoll said. "That involves chemistry, which I was never any good at. Now that you mention it, though, there's a fellow at the university who teaches chemistry. I guess I'll keep the calculator to give to him."

"If the notebook has no power, why did Bonder want it?" Benjaric asked.

"I assume, because he thought it was some kind of magical charm, or his superiors did. I don't think these cultists are quite bright."

"But they apparently chased you down just to get it. That means somebody in the Carche cult, or maybe both cults, knew you were going to find it, or somehow knew the moment you did find it," Benjaric said.

Hondoll was silent a while, then said, "You're right. Come to think of it, I had a premonition I was going to find it. I hadn't quite put it together. I don't have any good answers for that."

"Barrceil, please continue," the King said. Barrceil told her story, with additions from Fanward.

"This seems a little pat," Benjaric commented. "Barrceil gets captured, then rescued by Fanward from a bad man she didn't even see, and now Fanward sits in the presence of the King. If the Carche cult was trying to infiltrate the palace, wouldn't they do just this? How do we even know this man is a magician?"

"Well, that's easy enough to test," Hondoll said. "Fanward, do a trick."

"Stop!" Benjaric said instantly. "Is that safe?" He stood and summoned his men back into the room. They stood with swords out.

"I have already erected protections for the King," Hondoll said. Leovar had remained at his ease and had not moved. "I will make them visible." He spoke a spell out loud and traced the diagram, and the King was surrounded by a shimmering cylinder in the air.

"But you have already said that the cultists can nullify magic," Benjaric said sharply.

The King's voice was not hampered by his magical shield. "If it is true that this so-called 'god' can do anything, then we are already lost. Let's go on the assumption that Carche and the other one are not omnipotent. Goodman Fanward, do you know the little spell for hanging lights in the air?"

"Yes, sir," Fanward said.

"Hondoll, please signal if Fanward attempts any other spell. Goodman Fanward, show us that, please." Fanward spoke aloud the mathematical expression for his spell, using precise diction from which all of his rustic accent was suddenly missing. He traced the diagram of morphisms with one finger before him. Three bright sparks of light formed in the air and rose above his head, circling slowly near the ceiling of the room. Fanward put his hands down and sat silently.

Hondoll caused the cylinder around the King to fade back to invisibility. "There you are, general. Fanward is a magician."

"He could have memorized a few spells," Benjaric said.

"No, sir," Hondoll said. "General, people who are not in my field often misunderstand this. The mathematics you studied in school is based on *abstraction*. In other words, two beers plus two more beers makes four beers. Two of anything plus two more makes four of those things. So we abstract away all of the irrelevant details and just say that two plus two equals four, which covers all cases. The real world vanishes, and we can get useful results just by manipulating the symbols according to rules. Math is much simpler than messy reality."

He looked around. "Usually, the first thing that gets abstracted away is the person of the mathematician. Before the Deluge, everyone believed that mathematics always works, no matter who does it. But Offand found an exception, the first one in the whole history of numbers. In magical mathematics, the mathematician cannot be abstracted away from the math. Magic never works except when wielded by a mathematician who understands it, at a very thorough level. It's not a question of getting a university degree – Fanward here learned it from books, and so can anyone with his admirable tenacity. It just requires native wit, study and lots of work. So we can be sure that Fanward really understands mathematics, which means that he is a magician. Now, please understand that he can be a magician and also be a bad man – I can't guarantee against that. But I don't think he is, and neither does Barrceil."

"Fanward," the King said, "*are* you a good man?"

Fanward said simply, "Yes, sir."

The King said, "General Benjaric, I appreciate your concern but Hondoll has acted as a bodyguard for me many times and I trust his skill. Please ask your men to wait outside again." Benjaric waved, and the soldiers filed out.

"I wish it were easier to train magicians," the King commented. "I can never hire enough for my staff, not to mention the military. Fanward, later come talk to me about what we can do to find students like you and get them into the right schooling. But let's get back to business. Hondoll, when you told me you were going to search for that notebook, I told you to get in and out inconspicuously and not attract attention. You tell me that notebook is not important in itself, but I'm not convinced. You and I are going to have a discussion about your actions later. But putting that aside, how in the *hell* does the King's Magician get captured and held by a bunch of religious soft-brains? How is that even possible? Were you napping?"

"Something was suppressing my magic," Hondoll said. "You understand, speaking the spell and tracing the runes in the air, that's intended to help the magician concentrate. It's not required. The only thing that is actually necessary to effect a spell is for the magician to have the will to do it and the concentration to understand the math involved. I was working mentally, trying to free myself with magic the whole time, and failed. I'm sure they would have dissolved my disguise spell on the notebook if anybody in that room had had the brains to think of it. They have some … some *thing* to make magic less potent."

"There are spells that work on other spells," Barrceil said. "Could they have had someone wielding one of those?"

"It's possible," Hondoll said. "I've never had any occasion to use them myself, but all of my spells are constructed to be resistant to that kind of interference – that's just doing a workmanlike job. I can't rule out that somebody has developed some new suppressing spell, I suppose. But who?"

"Rendenen?" Barrceil asked. The King looked from one to the other.

"He works for Panhegan now," Hondoll said. "If it was him, Bonder wouldn't have had his spell. Besides, Rendenen is good but not that good – he's competent, but not up to Barrceil's level, nor mine. I don't think he could formulate a spell like that. I've met every really first-rank theoretical magician in the kingdom, read all their papers, and I can't think of one who could develop such a thing."

"Do you think it's the power of this god? Something different from magic?" Leovar asked.

"I suppose I can't rule that out," Hondoll said reluctantly. "But in my field, people are always trying to get us to accept supernatural craziness. I can't take these cheapjack silly gods seriously. And if it was a power from the real God, I think He'd give it to somebody more sensible."

"My King," Fanward began, and waited for

the King to acknowledge him. When Leovar nodded, he began again, "My King, the priests of Carche can wield some of the god's power, and magic is unreliable near them. I tried some little tests with their permission, and my magic failed. They had to withdraw their suppression from my boat before Erstone could lift and move it by magic."

"Thank you, Fanward," the King said. "You know, these groups have been around my whole life as little secret mystery cults. Nobody ever paid them much attention. The Carche people were just drunkards who wanted to play at being exalted, and the Panhegan people were self-righteous prigs, and there were always a few other mysteries and loose-minded new religions to take money from the credulous. Why have they grown so bold now? Hondoll, I think you were associated with Carche when you were in college?"

"I loved Rendenen," Hondoll said. "He was a freshman when I was a boy prodigy – we were younger than everyone else in the Math department. When he fell in with the Carche cult, I followed him, for a while. But I never saw anybody at their meetings who seemed to be competent at anything, except Rendenen himself. They just drank, and sang hymns, and fornicated. I never thought for a moment that they would actually be capable of … well, of anything like what just happened to me."

"Fanward, your experience is more recent.

Tell us about the Carche cult," the King said.

"Sir," Fanward said after a long pause, "I am estranged from my family now that I have left the cult, and that Erstone raped my daughter. I hate everything they stand for … but I was a worshiper, and I have to tell you, some people really do become saintly and exalted in the worship of Carche. I think, now, the priests are evil, but not all of the followers are. Carche does bring something to them."

"Do you know why they are extending themselves and snatching my ministers now?"

Fanward looked up in surprise. "Why, of course, sir. They have told everyone, when they parade through the city with their bands and signs. Both the Carche and Panhegan faiths."

"I have not paid attention," the King said dryly. "Tell me."

"The Birth-Day is coming," Fanward said. "The Winter Solstice, December 21. Carche will be born that day, unless Panhegan prevents it. They say Panhegan will be born the same day, unless Carche can block him."

"And then what will happen?"

"That will be the end of the world."

"Well," the King said cheerfully, "I think we can all agree that it's my duty, as steward of the realm, to prevent the end of the world. For one thing, I wouldn't be able to collect taxes – we can't have that! Fanward, do you know any of the details?"

"All of the adherents of Carche are required

to go to the town of Dry Harbor in the days before that date, because that was where the Sorcerer's Deluge began and where the god will be born. I have heard that Panhegan has issued a similar decree. I don't know any further details."

"We'll have to prevent them from doing that," Leovar said. "They fight each other now when their parades and pageants happen to meet in the streets. If thousands of them all go to Dry Harbor, there will be riots and bloodshed. They'll probably wind up burning the town down. General Benjaric, we will meet stupid actions with smart force. Take as many troops and horse as necessary from all regions, to make sure this gathering does not take place. Do we know how many of these cultists there are?"

"My intelligence officer says about twelve thousand across the kingdom, sir," Benjaric said.

"And in other countries? Would they all try to get to the same town?"

"I don't know," Benjaric said, frowning. "I'll find out. But sir, why not just defend Dry Harbor with magic? Erect a barrier around the town and not let outsiders in?"

The King looked at Hondoll. "It's what I was saying about magic requiring the presence of the magician," Hondoll said. "Magical expressions are equations that have two solutions. One of them contains coefficients that are commotic numbers, so we don't know what it affects. But the other one is a vector that goes in the direction of what the magician is looking at or visualizing. I know, it's strange. That's why nobody discovered it before Offand. I can make a barrier wherever I am, like the one that protects the King right now, but I can't make a wall around a town because only the part I could see directly would exist. The rest would vanish as soon as I left the area. We could build such a wall with many magicians, but we don't have that many."

"And besides, we know that at least the Carche priests can penetrate your barriers," Benjaric said. "Probably the Panhegan priests, too. What can we do to secure that town?"

"We can use all the tools we have," the King said. "We will use magicians, we will use military force, we will build walls, we will use the Civic Guard and we can use persuasion. Magic is not … well, it's not 'magic' in the sense of having unlimited power. Sometimes brute force is more powerful than magic, and sometimes public opinion is, too. If we combine them all together, we are more powerful than these damn-fool cultists." He turned to Hondoll. "As far as you, Hondoll, I'm not sure how to make use of you. I trust you, but frankly, I'm not sure how far I can trust your magic, now. One thing I want you to do is move into your castle. I want you in a secure place, guarded by troops. You're too valuable to risk. Doctor Barrceil, Goodman Fanward, please stay with Hondoll. I'll provide some funds to compensate you."

"You have seen the weapons spells I can

wield, sir," Hondoll said. "I'm sure I can help defend Dry Harbor."

"I'm well aware of what you can do," the King said with a cold smile. "I would prefer to do this without killing any more of my subjects than necessary, especially poor, deluded, superstitious fools. Let's see if we can do this by persuading the cultists not to meet in Dry Harbor."

"My King ..." Fanward began. At Leovar's nod he continued, "My King, the passion Carche inspires is very deep. His followers will not listen to reason. I expect the followers of Panhegan are about the same."

The King nodded. "Hondoll," he said, "there are spells of persuasion that can change a person's opinions, I think?"

"Yes, sir," Hondoll said. "But as we saw in Dry Harbor, it's not worthwhile to use them on more than a few people at a time."

"General Benjaric?" the King asked. "How many cultists just in River's Lover?"

"Perhaps two thousand, between both cults," Benjaric said.

"We can compel the cultists to come to the city square," the King said to Hondoll. "That many will just fill it, I think. Suppose you and all the other magicians I can assign try to persuade them using spells, to stay away from this 'Birth-Day,' a few people at a time for each magician? Failing that, perhaps we can persuade them with reason. If *that* fails, let's try to persuade them with fear. I will deploy heavy cavalry. In fact, I'll be there to lead the Army myself."

The King smiled more amiably and continued, "I'm thinking you are good at lectures. You certainly lecture *me* often enough! Perhaps you could deliver a lecture for an hour. How long would you need to prepare?"

"Not long," Hondoll said ruefully. "As you say, I'm full of lectures."

"Then prepare a lecture on some topic, and we will ensure your audience. We'll do this in the evening two weeks from now."

Hondoll nodded.

Six

Hondoll had a vast and gloomy castle by the edge of Stara Forest, which he preferred never to use because it was vast and gloomy. He better enjoyed his comfortable, book-lined apartment in the city. But obedient to the King, he had moved into his quarters in the castle.

The roof of the castle was flat, bordered with a low crenelated wall. It was a good place for Hondoll to be alone, pacing back and forth to think. The night was cold, and he was forced to wear his heavy, impressive wizard's robe just to stay warm. Like the castle, the robe was a gift from the King, and also like the castle, it had been given to Hondoll to serve the King's needs, not his own.

The castle was an old relic of a war between two nations whose lands had long since been absorbed into the kingdom. The King had no military use for it, but its square thick towers and massive brickwork made a good backdrop to show off the King's mighty wizard. A few times a year, the King would send various noblemen, foreign dignitaries and court officials to be entertained by Hondoll at the castle. All of them were chosen because the King felt they needed a lesson about the King's power. Hondoll would come out from the city, dress up in his robe and perform terrifying demonstrations of destructive magic for the benefit of his audience. The grounds around the castle were blackened and riven by fire, lightning, flood and cracking cold.

When his guests were suitably awed, they would leave and Hondoll would go back into town to study and read.

He looked down now over the parapets, at the dim expanse of Stara Forest and at the soldiers deployed by the King to guard him. They paced back and forth between bright lights of magic maintained by military magicians. Inside the guard lines, there were flickering lights of ordinary charcoal fires, set to help keep the soldiers warm.

Barrceil opened the vestibule door of the stairway that led up to the roof. She had found a wool coat and a knit cap, under which her bright hair peeked out. "Hondoll," she said, "are you all right?"

"I'm fine. Is something wrong?"

"I'm not sure. Something smells bad-magical. Mind if I come up to join you? Or do you want to be alone?"

"I wanted to be alone," Hondoll said, "but it's not working, so sure, come on up. Maybe you can help me. I'm trying to think of something to do about preventing this 'Birth-Day' melee but my mind really doesn't work that way."

"You know," Barrceil said, smiling, "people in the math department at school had a reputation for being able to dampen any party. Maybe we could work the same magic on their 'Birth-Day' gathering?"

"I don't think that was magic, I think it was our sparkling personalities," Hondoll said, returning her grin. "But now that you mention it, the cults surely do enjoy getting together in crowds and generating crowd energy. Is there some morphism we could write that would make them averse to crowds?"

"We're both pretty introverted," she said. "If anybody could understand how to generate that feeling, it would be us."

"Creating a longing for solitude and reflection," Hondoll mused. "If I could do that, I can see a lot of applications."

The air began to spin on one corner of the roof. It thickened into a little "dust devil," became opaque, and suddenly popped like a soap bubble. Rendenen stood before them, wearing a warm wool coat and with his shaven head covered with a knit wool cap.

"Yes, I smelled this coming," Barrceil said quietly.

"Hello, Rendenen," Hondoll said quietly. "I thought I had guarded the place against any intruder, bad or good."

"Hello, Hondoll. I wield some of the power of Panhegan, which can overcome magic. As you know," Rendenen said, and turned to bow to Barrceil. "Barrceil, I'm glad you're all right. It's nice to see you again. It's been a long time."

"It has," she said. "Rendenen, you are not here to do us harm, are you?"

"Not at all. I am here to do you a wonderful service, in fact."

"You're going to give us the missionary pitch for your god, right?" Hondoll said. "Rendenen, you tried that on me when you were excited about Carche. Did it ever work then?"

"I was wrong then," Rendenen said easily. "Carche is false, Panhegan is true. Truth and rectitude are always stronger than error and licentiousness. I know better now. But Hondoll my friend, no one is ever brought to truth about God by argument. When Panhegan reaches out to your heart, you will be convinced, and not before that moment."

"I wish you would say 'a god' instead of 'God,'" Barrceil said. "We already acknowledge the authority of God."

"To be sure, the big fellow," Rendenen said. "The one nobody sees, nobody ever talks with except inside their own heads. Barrceil, we acknowledge that God too, but my dear, we are only human beings. We are small, stupid, weak in our faith, not good for much without divine help. The big God is too austere and remote for us. We need a local god we can see and hear. We need Panhegan, who will be the visible presence of God here and will accept our worship on His behalf. You, and you, Hondoll, you need to come before Panhegan with an open heart."

"Okay, you've made your pitch," Hondoll said. "Now what?"

"Don't be hostile," Rendenen said. "I saved

61

you from the Carche fanatics, didn't I?"

"Forgive me if I believe you had another motive besides my welfare," Hondoll said. "What do you think I can do for Panhegan? If he is a god, he can will things into existence. I am limited to what I can do with magic, or with my hands like any other man."

"But in fact, he cannot will himself into existence," Rendenen said. "He will be brought into existence by the worship of his people, on the Birth-Day."

"If he has not yet come into existence, how can you exploit his power?"

"Panhegan is a god, and does not have the limits we imagine. When he is born three months from now, he will be able to reach back through time and create the initial conditions so that he will have existed since before the Earth was formed. Even now, he is not yet real but is becoming more and more real as he gains worshipers, and consequently his power becomes more and more available to me."

"That doesn't make any sense at all," Hondoll said peevishly. "That's just bibble-babble."

"You don't see the logic because Panhegan has not yet made himself manifest to you. When the god wills it, you will understand." Rendenen smiled and looked down, suddenly shy. "I'm looking forward to being on the same side with you," he said.

"Rendenen," Barrceil said, "what do you

actually want from Hondoll? Or me, for that matter?"

"I want your friendship," Rendenen said. "We were casual friends back in university, Barrceil, and I hope I can have at least that back again. Hondoll and I were close and I don't suppose I will ever have that level of affection from him again, but I do hope now for friendship."

"And?" Barrceil said.

"Well, first I have been sent to tell you that we see what you are doing with this 'public lecture' ruse, and it won't work. Hondoll, Barrceil, nobody knows better than you that those spells you plan to use on us don't convey any precise meaning. They induce *emotions*."

"So?"

"If you give those people an emotion of joy or love, they won't love the King, they will apply it to their god. If you give them hate, it will go toward the other cult. If you give them fear, they won't fear going to Dry Harbor, they will just panic. Sorrow will make them seek solace from their god. Honesty won't have any effect on them because they're already sincere. And if you try to enforce a spirit of servility, I think you can guess whose orders they will want to obey."

"Actually, I know that," Hondoll said. "But I'm thinking I'm skeptical of your so-called gods. Perhaps I can induce the crowd to be skeptical."

"Hondoll," Rendenen said with exasperation, "who are you talking to? Those

63

spells are published in the open literature and I can read them as well as you can. There is no spell to induce an emotion of skepticism, if it even is an emotion."

"We might try reason, without magic," Hondoll said mildly. "Actually, I would prefer that."

"All right, you always were stubborn. The High Priest has directed me to tell you that he will permit you to proceed with your lecture, and we have been informed that the Great Mother of the Carche cult feels the same."

Rendenen sat on the parapet wall and addressed them with grave friendliness. "I am also asked to tell you that the gathering for Birth-Day must occur. It is foreordained and Panhegan decrees it. Nothing can be permitted to stop it, and Hondoll, Barrceil, I mean that very sincerely. *Nothing* must obstruct that gathering, not the King, not the King's armies, and please, not either of you. I don't wish to threaten you" – he smiled, showing teeth – "but of course, I *am* threatening you. At the same time, Panhegan directs that the Carche cultists must not be permitted to gather."

"Why doesn't Panhegan enforce his desires himself?" Hondoll asked.

"Because he is not yet born," Rendenen said. "He needs our help until then, and wants our worship at all times. There is a third thing. I want – the High Priest wants – the Offand notebook. It does not belong to you."

"Rendenen, you, the High Priest and Panhegan can all go plow the beach," Hondoll said evenly.

Barrceil gestured toward the vestibule door as it opened to admit three of the King's military magicians to the roof. They stood in a line, ready and silent. "I asked them to come up if I did not make reassurances every so often," she said to Rendenen. "You are strong with some kind of power, but not stronger than all of us together, I think. Now quit your bullying and leave."

Hondoll held up a hand. "A moment, please. Rendenen, you can have my friendship again. You always could have had it. But one of the bonds we've had between us is mathematics, and math is stopped dead by contradiction. In all the fields of mathematics, over all the centuries, there has never been a contradiction because mathematics doesn't allow it, isn't that right? Now look, your god Panhegan, and your god Carche before that, is omnipotent, but he needs your help. He has power, but he isn't born yet. He wants your worship but he thinks you're stupid. How can you reconcile that with ... well, with the person I know you are? Come back, Rendenen."

Rendenen stood and regarded them all with an expression mixed of superiority and pity. "Everyone thinks he has the truth," he said. "But truth can be tested, and the test distinguishes what is consistent and what leads to contradiction. We will be tested, all of you and I, and we will see who has the truth."

Rendenen threw himself backward, over the parapet.

"Don't bother looking," Hondoll said. "He's transported himself home before he hit the ground. He always was a big show-off."

*   *   *

There was a windowless small room, previously a pantry, in the middle of the second floor of the castle. Hondoll sat in a hard chair with a little spark of magical light over his shoulder, trying to read Offand's notebook. He had physically locked the only door, then secured it with magic. He had fortified the room against the opening of magical portals, and in any case was sure that no one with magical skill had ever been in this musty room before and so could not visualize a portal into it. Guards were posted on all four sides of the room as well as on the floors directly above and below. Other guards, as well as magicians, patrolled the outside of the castle.

Hondoll drank from a glass of water, sat up in his chair and tried to apply himself to study and creative thought. After turning two pages of the notebook, he looked up and surveyed the stuffy, barren room, and shook his head with a sour look. It was not a place anyone would choose for study.

Seven

Fanward was disguised as a younger version of himself, but dressed in court clothes, dark and stylish. No one would see the resemblance between this smooth-cheeked fop and the weathered fisherman he really was. Hondoll had disguised himself with magic as well, giving himself the face of a boy who had bullied him when he was a teenager in school. The bully, backed by a gang of friends, had pushed him into a washroom stall and threatened to dunk his head in the toilet. Fortunately Hondoll had been rescued by a teacher, but in his terror he had never forgotten the bully's face, so it was easy for him to visualize it now for his spell: thick-lipped, plump, dark coarse hair and dark eyes. Hondoll wore the black and gray belted robe and trousers affected by the devotees of Panhegan.

They were sitting on a park bench, facing the Grand Temple of Panhegan, on a hill overlooking the river on the opposite bank from the King's palace. The building was huge and pretentious, and the Panhegan cultists were already entering the massive, carved-wood doors for First Day services.

"Let's wait until it's a little more full," Hondoll said. "We definitely want to be part of a big crowd."

"This makes me nervous," Fanward said. "If

we're discovered …"

"I've never been to one of their services," Hondoll said, "and I have got to know more about them. I mean, I can sort of understand people being attracted to Carche – drinking and orgies aren't for me, but a lot of people sure seem to enjoy them. But why would anybody sign up to be a repressed, sour prig?"

Fanward glanced at him sharply. "They get benefits out of it," he said. "Of course they do. They get to feel superior to everybody else, they get to believe they will be the ones who survive when the world ends, they get to be around people who will tell them they're doing right. Doctor Hondoll, you need to get out and meet people more."

"I suppose you're right," Hondoll said.

"Did you find anything in the Offand notebook?" Fanward asked.

"Not yet. At home I sit by the window to read, I can hear the sounds coming up from the city square, I've got sunlight and hot tea or cold beer. Trying to concentrate in that airless little pantry is pretty terrible. It's like sitting in a shipping crate. It's secure but I can't think well. There were a couple of interesting ideas in the part of the notebook I've read so far, but I sure don't see why the cultists are interested in it."

"I don't think the line's going down," Fanward commented. "We probably should just get in it." They got up and walked across the street to the temple. Men and women were in different queues, and looked at each other without conversation. They joined the end of the men's queue. Aside from dressing in gray and black, the people in line looked entirely ordinary.

Their attempt at blending in did not work for ten seconds. The plump, gray-haired man ahead of them turned back and said, "Hello! You're new here, aren't you? Welcome! If you haven't heard the good news Panhegan brings, you'll be blessed today."

Hondoll and Fanward looked at each other. "We ... we just wanted to come in and hear the service," Hondoll said. "I hope that's all right."

"It's fine! We get visitors every day. You're wearing gray and black but not the same way we do. I can always tell."

The line moved up a few places. Finally Fanward said, "Why do you wear gray and black, sir?"

"Because we're mourning all of those who will die on the Birth-Day," the man said, beaming. "All the sinners and non-believers and sun-worshipers and those horrible Carche people. But that won't be me and it won't be you if you turn your life to the right path. You can do that today! In fact, I'm sure you will do it."

"I'm looking forward to the service," Hondoll said insincerely.

"Oh, nobody enjoys the first time," the man said cheerfully. "But it will do your soul good. The blessing comes when it's over."

"I beg your pardon?" Hondoll said.

They reached the door of the temple. The gray-haired man disappeared into one of several dark doorways. An usher grabbed Hondoll and sent him into another. Fanward was sent in a different direction.

Hondoll found himself in a black, unlit room. He could touch both walls. He turned to go back out and found the exit blocked. He used a spell to create a light, and it failed. He tried spells to open a portal, to break walls, to talk to others, all without results.

At the same time, a terrible emotion of desperation came on him, driving him to find an exit. The panic came on him so suddenly that he suspected manipulation, but his mind was so distracted he could no longer formulate a counter-spell. He bumped into the walls with his hands before him, and blindly stumbled into an opening to another black room.

When he entered that room, the opening vanished behind him.

He bumped and groped through room after room, always alone, always despairing and fearful. In each tiny room, one exit opened and the previous entrance closed. Hondoll was crying with fear and, he suddenly realized, loneliness. He wanted company more than life, more than light.

Room followed room followed room, leading Hondoll on a crooked path. Each room was not only lightless but soundless: Hondoll did not make an audible thump with any of his increasingly erratic collisions. He yelled but the sound was absorbed.

At the end, frantic and wailing, he fell through a doorway into a large, bright room walled with stained glass windows. A dozen men were there to pick him up, hug him and surround him as he was guided to a chair. Hondoll clung to them desperately, sobbing. The men patted his shoulders and comforted him, and one brought him a cup of water.

Eventually Hondoll caught his breath enough to ask, "What happened to the man I came here with?"

"You don't need your old friends," the one who seemed to be the leader of the group said. "We are your friends now, and Panhegan loves you. You won't ever be lonely again."

Hondoll sat silently with tears on his face, stunned and helpless, clutching the arm of one of the men. He could not force himself to let go, to be separated from another person.

"Look at the pictures," the leader urged him gently, pointing to the stained glass. The light pouring through the windows was glorious with color. Hondoll obediently turned and regarded the images.

The windows showed young men and women dallying in sunlit gardens and formal lawns. The god Panhegan was depicted as a dragon floating overhead, gazing benignly on all. Each pane also had multiple copies of the same motif: the empty silhouette of a human body, outlined in black.

"When Panhegan brings the new world, you can live like us, like them," the leader said, pointing at the blessed. "Or you can be missing, a blank spot in the world, less than nothing, non-existent. Look at the empty outlines there – the non-believers, the worshipers of false Carche or the sun or any other thing. They will be as if they had never been born. But you can live. The difference is giving your love to Panhegan and following his precepts from now until the Birth-Day. Come with me."

The man held out his hand, and Hondoll took it and was pulled to his feet. Others had to steady him as he was led to the window and folded down onto a kneeling bar, facing the image of Panhegan. His head hung down, not from humility but from inability to hold it up.

"Great and Well-Loved Panhegan," the leader prayed, "open Doctor Hondoll's heart to the joy he could have ..." and continued for several minutes. Hondoll shook his head stupidly, and it gradually dawned on him that his disguise had been negated as well as his other spells. He wanted to get up and leave, and yet the thought of abandoning his new friends was too lonely to contemplate. He knelt while the leader droned on, his mind reeling. Gradually he raised his head up and looked at the glowing, stained glass picture of the dragon Panhegan.

His eyes were wide. He could not look away. He reached up to touch the image of the god with two shy fingers.

*   *   *

An hour later, the King himself rode up to the steps of the temple of Panhegan at the head of a force of twelve mounted soldiers and demanded Hondoll and Fanward. The cultists delivered them without protest. Both were staring and dazed. They were put into a carriage and brought back to the King's residence.

Eight

Barrceil rose from her chair beside the beds holding Hondoll and Fanward. "I can't do anything more right now," she said. "I've used some healing spells, but they need rest. We should let them sleep it off."

"When Hondoll came to me," the King said, musing, "he was still a boy. Very precocious, but very young. I still feel as though I need to protect him, even though he is also one of my fiercest warriors."

"I think they'll both be all right, but it will take a while," Barrceil said. "What kind of horrible initiation did they put them through, to leave them in this state?"

"The Great Mother of the Carche temple came to visit me this afternoon," the King said. "Stupid-looking woman, low and sly as a snake. She tried to convince me this outrage meant I should shut the Panhegan temple down. I just had her sent away."

"I'm pretty sure both sides will use you, or anything else at all, against the other," Barrceil said. "Let's go out and let these men alone for a while."

"I should post a guard," the King said. "There's no telling what will control Hondoll's mind when he wakes up. He may have been converted completely."

"If he has his magic back, no guard and no magician you have here could hold him against his will. But I think we can trust in his native sensibility. He was a boy when I met him too, even though he'd been admitted to the university." Barrceil paused and smiled, then continued, "A very pretty boy. All the girls in the math department were a little put out when he turned up with a boyfriend. But he was strong enough to hold his own among all the older students. He's still strong, and a good man. I don't think a couple of hours could break his character."

They retired to a sitting room in the King's quarters. The Queen came in and greeted her husband affectionately. She had their young daughter with her. The Infantessa was a little girl of six named Hoyeea, who was carrying a purse of wax crayons and a sheaf of paper she had been drawing on. She asked "Is Doctor Hondoll going to be all right?"

The King and Queen both looked at Barrceil, who turned to the girl and said, "Yes, dear. He'll be fine. He just needs to rest, and then he may need some medicine. But don't worry about him."

The Queen said, "She and Hondoll are great friends. He's known Hoyeea since she was born."

"I wish I knew magic," the girl said. "You know, to make him better."

"Doctor Hondoll will be all right," Barrceil said, smiling. "I do know healing spells, so I'll fix him up. But I'll tell you what. Do you want to learn a magic trick you can show him when he gets up? It'll make him laugh and feel better, I promise."

The little girl nodded. Barrceil stood, turned away from them with her hands behind her back and said, "All right. Take out some crayons of different colors but don't tell me what they are. You have that? Now put one in my hand where I can't see it. Good! Now look at the other crayons to make sure you know which one you gave me, then take the crayon back."

Barrceil turned, and raised up both arms, her fingers spread wide. "Oh, spirits of magic!" she intoned. "Give me mystical knowledge of things not seen! I invoke you with the magic word 'Ab-ra-ca-dab-ra!'"

Then she said, "Hold out the five crayons. Um, yes, the mystical knowledge is coming to me now. You gave me the red one, am I right?"

Hoyeea convulsed with laughter and said "Yes! How did you do that?"

"Why, I consulted with the mystical powers."

"My daddy says that's silly."

"You caught me! Your daddy's right. I'll tell you a secret, it's not really magic. Magic uses the arithmetic you're learning from your tutor. But if you learn to do this trick, you can show your friends and they'll all think you're a real magician. Want to know how?" Hoyeea nodded enthusiastically, and Barrceil continued, "When I had the crayon behind my back, I scratched it with my fingernail while I was talking to you, so I have a little red wax right here, see? Then when I put my arms out in front, I was still talking but I was looking at my finger and I could see the wax."

She continued, "Two things to remember. You have to practice this a lot so you can do it smoothly, and you have to keep talking the whole time. I think you're already good at that part, right?"

"Who can I practice on?" Hoyeea demanded.

"Your Mom and Dad," Barrceil said. "I guarantee they'll be surprised every single time you do it. After you've practiced on them, you can do it for your friends."

The Queen led her daughter out. When they had left the room, the King said, "Thank you, Barrceil. But how did you think of something like that?"

"I like to poke around the old stuff in the library. Hondoll and I used to do that together, actually. Anyway, one day I found an ancient, pre-Deluge book called 'Magic for Children,' and of course I had to read it. There wasn't any math at all in it. It was all slight-of-hand tricks like that one. I guess they used to have stage shows for 'magic' like that, although of course nobody bothers with that now. Anyway, I know some tricks that nobody expects now. Here, do you have a tenth-piece?"

The King indulgently reached into his purse

and handed her a coin. Barrceil bent her left arm and pointed to her loose sleeve. "Here, I'm going to drop this coin down my sleeve." She snapped her fingers and the coin vanished from her right hand. "Now, the coin's resting down by my elbow. I will magically pull it through the material," – she did that – "and now I can return it to you. My garment is untorn."

"You did use magic for that," the King said.

"No, sir. I snapped my fingers and you looked where my fingers were pointing. You thought the coin went into my sleeve but it actually stayed in my hand all along."

"Do that again." Barrceil went through the same routine, obviously well-rehearsed, and the King laughed and said, "I would swear you dropped that coin. Well done! But couldn't you do that with real magic?"

"I'd have to have an accomplice," she said. "Any magician can change the location of an object that he can see, but the diagram is too complicated to sketch while I'm holding the coin. So one person would have to hold the coin and seem to do the trick, and other one would invoke the spell from the back of the room or something. Too much work for some very unimpressive magic. I just use these tricks with children."

The King looked thoughtful. "I've seen Hondoll destroy buildings, raise floods, melt iron and so forth," he finally said. "My idea was for him to awe the cultists into submission, or change their emotions while they were distracted.

But if the cultists can nullify magic, that's not going to work."

"I'm pretty sure they can't all do it, just the priests and trained magicians like Rendenen," Barrceil said. "I think suppressing magic is probably like doing magic – the person doing it has to be looking at the place where the effect will happen. But do they have any magic of their own? Maybe they can hinder magic but not do anything magical themselves. So they don't have any protection against swords and cannon."

"Both cults have some magicians, and for all I know they have swords and cannon of their own, too," the King said fretfully. "I finally sat down to look at those intelligence reports Benjaric's men have prepared. They're worthless. Nobody's been able to infiltrate into either cult. Anyone we send in, becomes a believer and their reports are lies. We don't really know anything."

"Hondoll left the Carche cult, and so did Fanward. There must be other ex-members we could learn from."

"Hondoll, as you say, has a very firm character. Fanward had his family trauma to loosen him. My intelligence men haven't been able to turn up anybody lately who has left the cults. They think the influence the cults have on their members is stronger than it was a few years ago."

"Because they're getting closer to the 'Birth-Day'?" Barrceil asked gently.

"It's hard to tell what's real and what's just

blathering," the King said. "They brought me some of the publications from both cults, and they're complete nonsense, just words that don't go together. I hate to put any stock in their stupid theologies but I don't know what might be real."

"Well," Barrceil said, "according to Rendenen, they'll let Hondoll's lecture go on. Maybe he can talk some sense into them, or at least scare them. I need to get back to the university library. I know where there are some books that might help."

"Before you magic yourself out of here," the King said, "let's go look in on Hondoll and Fanward."

But when they went back to the room, both beds were empty.

Nine

Hondoll opened his eyes to see the dayroom of his own castle, with couches and comfortable chairs, a table with books on it, pictures on the wall. Rendenen was there, sitting pensively by the window looking out, his face highlighted by sunlight from one side. Hondoll watched him silently a moment, until Rendenen turned his head. Hondoll sat up.

"I took away all the emotional manipulation, the loneliness and all," Rendenen said immediately. "For you and the other fellow there. You should be fine now, except for maybe a headache."

"Why did you transport us here?" Hondoll asked.

"I figured you'd recover faster in familiar surroundings," Rendenen said.

"So you invited yourself into my castle. Wonderful." Hondoll turned back to see Fanward, who was still unconscious on the other couch. He let him sleep.

"Who did this to us in the Panhegan temple?" Hondoll asked.

"I did," Rendenen said. He slid down from the window seat and took a chair closer to the couch on which Hondoll was sitting. "My friend, I'm sorry. I really am. I've been callous. I set up that maze to prepare new worshipers for

Panhegan, but until I saw what it did to you, I never really thought much about what effect it was having. I wish you hadn't gone through that."

"I wish I hadn't, either," Hondoll said. He reached idly across the table in front of him and picked up one of the books, then put it on the couch next to him. He examined his own mind, running through standard tests memorized by all magicians, and concluded that he had no lingering emotional effects from his trauma. He finally said, "When I'm upset and hurt and I have problems, my mind always wants to divert me into technical questions."

Rendenen smiled. "I know," he said gently. "You were always that way."

"How did you apply that spell in a room you couldn't see, because it was pitch black?"

"I explored that maze with the lights on," Rendenen said, "and then was careful never to go back in when it was dark, so I can visualize the rooms without experiencing it the way you did. I was upstairs having tea with the Arch-priest while you were there. I never paid attention to who was actually going through the maze, didn't know it was you until later."

"How were you able to keep me from using magic?"

"I have been given some power by the Archpriest," Rendenen said. "Not as much as a priest, but I have some ability to suppress magic."

"How does that work?" Hondoll demanded.

"I don't know. It's a mystery, even to me, even to the Archpriest. We'll know more after the Birth-Day."

"Did you work a spell on me for religious adoration? That's new."

"Yes. I developed that myself," Rendenen said. "I haven't published it or anything."

"Man, I'm hopeless," Hondoll said ruefully after a moment, "My first reaction is, I'd like to look at your math on that spell." He straightened up, then continued, "Rendenen, you were converted to Panhegan without that spell, and I presume everybody in the cult before you got there was. Why do you think it's all right to manipulate people that way?"

"It brings them to rectitude and truth, which means they will live. Everyone who is not a follower of Panhegan will die. I can't apologize for that."

"And yet you released me from the spell."

Rendenen sighed and looked down. "I did. I suppose I want you to accept the Unborn God the way I did, not in some artificial way. Please, you need to do it before the Birth-Day. Don't wait too long."

"That's touching," Hondoll said. "If you hadn't practically damn near killed me and my friend, I'd be even more touched."

Fanward began to stir. Hondoll went to him, took a cup from the mantlepiece, caused water to pour out of the air into it, and gave it to Fanward when he sat up. "We're back in my castle," he said quietly. "Fanward, this is Rendenen, he's … an old friend. He extracted us from the King's quarters and released us from the spells he put on us in the first place."

"Hello," Fanward said, and added nothing. He clutched the water and drank it down.

"Fanward is a self-taught amateur magician," Hondoll said. "He's a fisherman."

Rendenen smiled with genuine warmth. "I'm glad to meet you," he said. "I always learn something new from the self-taught. We never have enough of them. That's admirable."

"Wait a moment, people will be worried about us," Hondoll said to both of the other men. He invoked a spell to connect his voice to both the King and Barrceil. After a few moments of conversation, he said to Barrceil, "I don't think he means us harm. He managed to evade my guards coming here but I can call for help if I need it, and I've got Fanward. Don't worry about us." Presently he relaxed the connection.

"I have to tell you, if you hold that silly 'lecture' the King wants, the Archpriest will be there to interfere with any magic you attempt," Rendenen said.

"Will you be there to interfere as well?" Hondoll asked.

Rendenen looked down, looked up and said, "No. I won't interfere. I won't oppose you. But Hondoll, if you actually convince anybody away from Panhegan, you're sending them to die."

"Stop that. Rendenen, you're out of your mind. I sure wish I could talk to the Rendenen I used to know. The old Rendenen, he could argue better than I could and he could talk you out of this nonsense. But anyway, I think I know the way out of this problem. I'll bring in more magicians. Whatever power your Archpriest or all his little priests have, it's not unlimited. If I have enough magicians working to support me, I can do whatever magic I need."

"Doctor Hondoll," Fanward said, "two things I can tell just from looking at your two faces. First, you two used to be lovers, and there's still something left of that. For both of you, I mean, and you can't hide it. Second, he thinks you're being foolish about the lecture."

"You always were a cocksure little rooster," Rendenen said bitterly. "You thought you were the smartest person in the room, every time."

"Well, as far as I know, I always was," Hondoll said.

"I'll be going now," Rendenen said, standing. "Fanward, good to meet you. I hope you'll let me talk to you about virtue and leading a moral life sometime. I don't think boy-genius here wants to hear that conversation. Hondoll, you're ..." He stopped, unable to finish. He spoke a spell and gestured to open a portal in front of him, then turned and grinned at Hondoll. "Read any good books lately?" he asked genially. With a quick grab, he took the book off Hondoll's couch, then stepped through his portal before Hondoll could react.

"What did he take?" Fanward asked.

"A copy of the Offand notebook," Hondoll said. "I duplicated it so I could read it here where I'm comfortable."

"Weren't you going to keep the only copy locked up?"

"I thought nobody would notice," Hondoll said bitterly. "That *thief!*"

Ten

The central square of the city of River's Lover was called the Midst. On a pleasant early evening with the sun going down among clouds, The Midst was filling rapidly. Adherents of Carche came in from the east side and followers of Panhegan from the west side. Civic Guardsmen on horses patrolled restlessly up and down aisles of people sitting on the pavement or on cushions, keeping the two factions apart. They had not permitted anyone to bring chairs, for fear the furniture would be used as weapons.

At the north end of the Midst, Hondoll sat with the King and the royal family, who did have chairs. "They have their families, see?" he said complacently. "No parent is going to risk exposing their children to what I'm going to show them. This will be just the excuse they need to stay away from Dry Harbor."

The King looked at him sourly. "The two leaders are both here," he said. "We know one of them can suppress magic, probably the other can, too. They have their magicians here as well, and a lot of sturdy men."

"But we have thirty-eight trained magicians, plus ground troops and horse companies," Hondoll said. "We have reason and the law on our side. I'm sure the great majority of them have never seen the kind of magic I'm going to show them."

When the square was full, Hondoll went and conferred with his contingent of the King's staff magicians, military magicians and his magician friends, including both Barrceil and Fanward. They dispersed to positions around the square. Translucent, impassable barriers of magic formed between the Carche and Panhegan sides, low enough to permit everyone to see the stage but obviously ready to be raised higher at need.

Hondoll climbed the steps to the platform on the north end of the square, stood in front of the chair placed there. The sun was low, and he quietly spoke a spell to create a thousand small points of light in the air above, circling like slow fireflies. Another spell distributed his voice so that he could speak intimately to each person without amplification.

"My Sovereign King Leovar, my Queen Spartria, Infantessa, welcome, and thank you for allowing me to be here this evening," he said, with a bow to the box next to the platform. With a bow that was precisely a little less deep, he gave his respects to various lords and ladies of the court. He exchanged a glance with Barrceil, standing near the platform, and she looked back without speaking.

Hondoll turned to face the square and said, "I am Hondoll, the King's Magician. Welcome to you all, and thank you for attending! We have with us tonight two very special guests. On the left side of the square, His Eminence the

Archpriest of the Unborn God Panhegan."
Hondoll waved gracefully to indicate the
Archpriest, but was unable to keep a small edge
of sarcasm out of his voice. The Archpriest, a
stern-faced man resplendent in robes and
surrounded by his priests, nodded very slightly.

Hondoll turned the other way, and said with
even more evident sarcasm, "On the right side of
the square, we welcome the Great Mother
Repallinia, Speaker for the Unborn God Carche."
The Great Mother gave a frosty nod as well. Her
followers glared at the worshipers of Panhegan,
who returned the looks equally.

"To the followers of Carche and Panhegan,"
Hondoll said, "I realize that you have been
'invited' here by King Leovar, with the invitation
worded in such a way that you dared not refuse.
There is a reason for this, which I will detail in a
little while, and I promise you that you will find
my talk useful and, I hope, also interesting."

He paced the stage. Quite aside from his
tightly controlled gestures as a magician, Hondoll
also had a habit of talking with his hands, and he
waved them as he walked. "I am the King's
Magician. I serve my liege King Leovar with
love and loyalty, and I am a defender of our
nation against all who would do us harm. My
topic tonight is, 'Where Does Your Lap Go When
You Stand Up?'"

The audience stirred, unable to decide
whether this was a joke or not. Hondoll smiled
amiably and said, "I know, I know, that's not the

title that was announced. You have come here to hear a lecture on 'The Mathematics of Magic' and to those who came here willingly to hear such a dry topic, my grateful thanks. But I want to begin by asking the Infantessa to come out and help me. For those of you who are wondering, of course I am not offering the King and Queen a surprise – anyone knows better than to do that! We have discussed this beforehand, you can be sure."

Hondoll turned to the King's box. "Infantessa Hoyeea, will you ask your mother and father if you can come out here to help me? And please bring your dolly." The little girl conferred with her parents and then was escorted out of the box and on to the platform by her disapproving nurse. Hondoll greeted her with grave courtesy and she, already regal at the age of six, nodded to him.

"Where does your lap go when you stand up?" Hondoll said to the audience. He pulled his chair toward him and sat down. He picked up Hoyeea gently and sat her on his lap. She held her doll in her own lap as well. "Please observe that I am holding the Infantessa on my lap. Are you comfortable, dear? This won't take long. All of you will appreciate that this is a position of some peril to me. The Infantessa might fall off my lap to the floor. You know, and believe me that I know, that if I were to offer any indignity to the King's daughter, he would react with the anger any father would show. But I can hold the

Infantessa confidently, secure in the knowledge that my lap is easily able to support her."

Here Hondoll paused for an aside to the little girl that his audience did not hear. "Hoyeea," he whispered, "may I tell the people your dolly's name?" She looked wide-eyed and shook her head wildly.

"You will note that the Infantessa holds her doll," Hondoll continued to the audience, "on her lap. That's a point I want to go back to later. Now that I have demonstrated my lap, I can set my princess down." He did so and whispered to her again, and she ran back to her nurse.

Hondoll stood. "Now I stand up, and I no longer have a lap. Think about that for a moment. Isn't that odd? My lap existed, and it was strong enough to suspend the Infantessa above the floor, against the force of gravity. Now it does not exist. We have an expectation in daily life, don't we, that something that exists should continue to exist? More formally, we have scientific laws of the Conservation of Matter and the Conservation of Energy. These laws are taught in all schools and at the University here in the city, they have been tested myriads of times and no exception has ever been found. And yet now, I have just made something to exist, and then caused it not to exist again. And although I am a magician, please believe me when I say that no magic was used!" This time the people were confident that he had attempted a joke, and tittered a little.

"Both the King and I are adherents of the

Afsteric Aesthetic, a school which emphasizes rationality and logic. This school does not require materialism, but many of us are effectively materialists." He smiled at the audience and mentioned in a lower voice, "I have never understood the concept of 'supernatural.' Nature is what exists. If something exists, it is part of nature. What can 'supernatural' possibly mean?"

He returned to his pacing. "However, there is a kind of stupid religion of materialism which is as stupid as … well, as whatever religion you think is stupid." The Carche and Panhegan cultists both audibly drew in their breaths, but Hondoll continued without pause. "Stupid materialism says that nothing exists but matter and energy, space and time. But matter is neither created nor destroyed – at least, not on Earth, not anymore. Some of you may know that things were different long ago, before the Sorcerer's Deluge. Energy is not created or destroyed. And yet you saw that I had a lap, reliable enough to let the Infantessa sit on it, and now I do not have a lap."

"This simple demonstration should tell you that some other thing exists in the world. My lap was made of matter – my own legs and trunk – but the matter is still here even though my lap is not. My lap was not itself matter or even matter-like. It was likewise not energy-like, space-like or time-like, and yet it existed. My lap, when I had it, was a *relationship*. Specifically, it was a relationship between various parts of my body, which existed as long as I was sitting and does not exist now that I am standing."

"So there is at least one other thing in the world besides matter and energy, space and time, and that thing is *relationships*. Now I want to go a step further and show you that relationships are the *only* important things that exist in the world," Hondoll said, and smiled again. "I can do this because you and I are in the relationship that I talk and you listen. Those of you who continue to listen by courtesy, thank you. Those of you who listen to me because you must, thank you also."

"Relationships. I am walking on the floor of a platform made of boards nailed together in such a relationship that I can stand a little way off the ground. The boards are made of wood, the wood is made of fibers that have the relationship of being entwined together, and the fibers are made of still smaller things. My body is similarly made of tissues, muscles, organs, bones, and everything that is needed to make a person. I live because they are all in very precise relationships to each other. Disturb almost any one of those relationships and I would die."

"We call the smallest particles of things 'atoms.' What are atoms that are not related to each other? They form a thin gas, worth nothing. If it were not for relationships, I would not be here to talk and you would not be here to listen. The world would be empty and stupid, even if it contained every atom that exists now. Only relationships are used to form the world and everything in it. Everything that exists is related to other things. If there was some thing that was not related to other things, it would not affect us in any way – how would we even know about it?"

"This is the secret of mathematical magic. I cannot make matter by magic, I cannot create energy. I don't know what it would mean to create space and time. But relationships are not any of those things, and are not bound by the laws that control them. There is no conservation law for relationships! Relationships do not have a well-defined position in space, they do not displace any air, they weigh nothing, they are not fixed in time. And yet, they are the fundamental stuff of the world."

"I can speak to each of you without straining or shouting, about two thousand of you, because I have used a magical spell that changes the relationship between my voice and your ears. The words that I speak are presented to you as though I were standing a few feet away, and I have made this happen to each of the two thousand of you as easily as I could with one person, because there is no rigor of conservation for relationships."

"The little lights above you are just openings through which the sun shines. My spell has found some place – some place I have been and am familiar with – where the sun is still shining, and has reset the relationships of a thousand little points to bring the light here."

"Magic is based on mathematical objects

called cantrips – 'cantrip' means 'a little trick' – and relationships called morphisms that act on them. Let me show you a little trick."

Hondoll spoke a spell and traced the diagram of its morphisms. A wavering patch of distorted air appeared before the face of each person in the audience. They leaned back and swatted at the patches as though they were insects, without effect. "This is a cantrip by itself," Hondoll said. "It's not very impressive, is it? It doesn't do anything much, it's almost useless. Most cantrips are similar."

He went back to his chair and sat. "A moment ago, the Infantessa was sitting on my lap, and her doll was sitting on her lap. Doesn't that mean that her doll could sit on my lap? [He smiled.] I mean, if she were willing to let go of it? In more mathematical terms, this is called transitivity and it means that if I have a cantrip that starts from A and creates an effect B, and another that goes from B to C, I can always write a spell that will go from A to C."

"Another property is composition. I can add cantrips together, and the combination has effects different from any of the original objects."

"Let me bring down the lights and move them to the sides of the square," he said, gesturing. He paused to speak a lengthy spell and trace an elaborate diagram. A plane, visible but transparent, formed in the air only a few feet above the heads of his audience. The plane extended to the limits of the square.

"The barrier above you will protect you from harm during my demonstration," Hondoll said. "Fear nothing. It is similar to the barriers that we have erected in the aisle to keep the two factions of believers apart. It establishes a relationship between a point in space and the point just next to that, such that light can go through it but any bit of matter that tries to pass finds itself heading in the opposite direction. In other words, nothing material can pass it. The evening is getting darker. Let's have some sunlight."

Over the square, the evening sky disappeared from above the barrier and was replaced by the sun shining down from a brilliant blue sky. The people, suddenly illuminated, looked at each other in fear. "This sky is taken from some other place in the world. I have not changed the sun, but I have changed the relationship between that bit of sky and here. I rather hope it's from some uninhabited part of the ocean, rather than frightening people in a town. As part of our education, magicians are always sent traveling widely, so that we have experience of all the places we might need to borrow something from. Now let's have more sunlight." At Hondoll's gesture, another image of the sun appeared in the sky, and the sunlight doubled. The heat grew intense.

"I have re-set the relationship between another place and this place, at the same time," Hondoll said quietly. "Now another." A third sun appeared above them, bringing triple sunlight.

The people began wailing and hiding themselves under their clothes. At Hondoll's gesture, the sunlight blinked out and the evening sky reappeared.

"There is no rigor of conservation for relationships," he repeated in the same tone. "If I need to do so to defend my King's lands, I can bring the sunlight from a hundred places to destroy any structure, any force raised against our nation. Did you know that at any moment, there are about ten thousand thunderstorms active on the Earth? I don't need to have visited every place where lightning might strike, because those lightning bolts are 'equal enough' to the ones I have seen and can visualize. Look up again, please." At his spell and gestures, lightning cracked from east to west across the sky. The thunder was instant and shattering.

"Snow," Hondoll said, and white flakes fell heavily on the barrier but did not pass it. "Rain," he said, and torrents fell from the empty sky, melted the snow and made a shimmering layer of water overhead. Hondoll let it remain above them.

"I have been sick in my life, so I know what the sensations of sickness are like," Hondoll continued, still quietly, "and I can give those sensations to anyone who threatens the peace of the kingdom. I can rob fire from forest fires and householders' fireplaces and bring it where it might be needed to stop a threat to peace. I can bring saltwater from the ocean, ice from the mountains, sand from the desert, bricks from ruined cities. All of these things I, and the King's other magicians, will wield to oppose anyone who threatens the peace of the Kingdom."

He raised the volume of his voice to a vast booming, although he did not shout. The sound echoed back from the buildings of River's Lover. "NOW LISTEN," he said.

"The King directs me to tell you that he considers the proposed 'Birth-Day' gathering in Dry Harbor to be a breach of the peace, and he will not permit it to occur."

"The King directs me to tell you that he considers the marches and rallies of followers of either Panhegan or Carche in this city to be breaches of the peace, and he will no longer permit them."

Hondoll's overhead barrier began to fail above him. Icy water trickled, then poured down on him. It also poured on the King and the nobility seated at that end of the Midst. Hondoll looked up, then hastily invoked a spell to re-establish the barrier. It did not work. The water flooded down.

On one side of the square, the Archpriest of Panhegan watched dispassionately, surrounded by cultists who guarded him effectively from the crowd. On the other side, the Great Mother also watched silently. The overhead barrier vanished completely, without wetting either of them.

The barrier running down the center of the Midst rotted into holes, was restored by Hondoll with a spell and gestures, then failed again. After a minute, it vanished completely, and the two cults joyfully gave battle to each other with fists and kicks. The horse-mounted Civic Guard rampaged among them, swinging clubs.

Both sides of the crowd surged toward Hondoll's corps of magicians. He watched in horror as the magicians were overwhelmed and knocked to the pavement. He realized bitterly that he had erred in stationing them at the sides of the crowd. He should have put them on balconies overlooking the Midst. As the King's Magician, Hondoll had always worked military magic while surrounded by troops to provide a buffer zone around him. He was sickened to realize he had overlooked the basic weakness of magical force: no magician could invoke spells without the mental calm to formulate and understand them. The howling, mindless attack of the crowds destroyed that. Some magicians were able to flee, some could fight back and a few were trampled unmoving to the pavement.

The crowd attacked the noble families too, and other cultists were rushing toward the King. Hondoll spun around as Barrceil rushed behind him to erect a barrier between the royal family and the rioters. It was melted away almost in the instant she made it. She and Hondoll jumped to put themselves in front of the Queen and little Infantessa, and the King drew his sword. Other guardsmen ran toward the approaching cultists.

Hondoll was able to open a portal to the

palace, but while the King was battling another swordsman – Hondoll had a moment of wonder that someone had been able to bring in a sword past the Civic Guard – a woman dived to the ground and slid forward to grab the Infantessa. Hondoll and Barrceil both leaped on them, and Barrceil was able to separate the Infantessa and thrust her through the portal while Hondoll wrestled with the woman. His battle ended when a guardsman stabbed the woman dead. Hondoll stood unsteadily and looked down at her body. She was dressed in green and yellow.

They managed to get the Queen through the portal unharmed, and the King pressed forward, bellowing and swinging his sword. He and his men were able to clear the space around them. Hondoll canceled the portal so that no cultist could run through it.

There was a building two stories high nearby. Hondoll looked at it and opened a portal to the roof, and he and Barrceil ran through it. From the roof, they were able to cast spells to make barriers between the rioters on each side, who were desperate in attacking each other, and between the rioters and nobles. The barriers sometimes worked, sometimes were canceled out.

Fires were started here and there, and apparently the priests approved of Hondoll's and Barrceil's actions in transporting water to flood them out, because those spells were allowed to work without hindrance.

The crowd had brought in stones with them. One was thrown directly up toward Hondoll's forehead and he was not alert to that attack. It knocked him back, reeling. Barrceil paused and worked a healing spell on him, then returned to her battle position at the edge of the roof while he recovered for a moment.

Barrceil called Hondoll to her and pointed. "Look who's leaving," she said. Hondoll could see the Archpriest of Panhegan rise, collect his entourage and walk away, apparently with the use of magic since they walked directly past a troop of Civic Guard without being noticed.

"So is the Great Mother," Hondoll said, pointing to the other side of the Midst. "Does that mean it's going to get calm or going to get worse?"

"We need to get our people up here." One by one, they located the fallen magicians and transported them, more gently than they had handled the rioters, up to the roof. Hondoll moved discarded cushions from the square to make bedding, and they laid the others out to be healed.

One of the magicians they retrieved, a middle-aged man Hondoll did not know well, was dead, beaten to death.

With the leaders gone, Hondoll's spells began to work more reliably. He dared not bring down any weather or calamity that would affect the troops as well as the cultists, so he contented himself with striking knots of rioters in his line of sight with nausea and bowel illness. The most heated fights began to break up.

The King, on horseback, led a sally directly down the middle of the square, splitting the two sides. Hondoll rebuilt the barrier behind him, from his rooftop, and this time the barrier held. The Civic Guard began to get the upper hand, and Hondoll turned back to help Barrceil with healing.

One magician cried and writhed on his cushions from internal wounds, while Hondoll worked magic over him. Hondoll could not heal injuries that his mind could not clearly visualize. The magician died even as his visible cuts and bruises began to knit, and Hondoll fell to his knees and wept.

Companies of regular Army cavalry arrived, filtering in through the side streets and forming ranks when they met in the Midst. The crowds fled down the side streets. In minutes, the riot was over.

Eleven

Hondoll fled to his castle and hid himself in books, particularly the Offand notebook. After some thought, he made more copies of the notebook and gave them to the King's staff magicians at the castle to study. He had always been generous about sharing his work with other mathematicians, not because he would not be annoyed if someone upstaged him but because he was egotistical enough to be sure no one would.

But for himself, he sat alone, pondering the Offand notebook and dreading the confrontation with the King that he knew was inevitable. He scribbled equations in his own notebook, scratched them out, tried out spells and gestures that resulted in dozens of useless little effects. His kitchen staff – the King's kitchen staff, he thought bitterly – put plates of food outside his door, which he ate. Anxiety had never affected his appetite.

On the third day, King Leovar came for him, leading a company of a dozen soldiers on horse. Hondoll humbly went downstairs and met him outside the door.

The King did not even dismount. He looked down at Hondoll and said, "I have waited until I could say this calmly, Hondoll. You were a boy genius and I was awed at your ability. I was proud to put you into my innermost staff. But you've used up that regard. You disobeyed my orders at Dry Harbor. You could not defend yourself against kidnapping by the Carche cult, which emboldens them against my rule. You tried to penetrate the Panhegan cult without consulting with me, allowed yourself and Fanward to be overwhelmed, and showed weakness before them. You exposed my wife and daughter to violence, and caused the death of two magicians and three soldiers, through your stubborn, arrogant and wrong belief in your own superiority. Hondoll, I do not tolerate incompetence and I do not order twice. Take what you own and leave this castle. You are not the King's Magician any longer."

"Your Majesty," Hondoll stammered, "I have discovered some hints in the Offand notebook that ..."

"Don't say it," Leovar said. "I don't trust what you say anymore. Go." Without a backward glance, he wheeled his horse around and the company started back toward the city.

Hondoll trudged back up to his residence and opened a portal to his apartment in the city, then carried in some books, clothing and miscellaneous stuff which he piled on the floor. He entered his apartment, looked back into the castle, then closed the portal behind him. He boiled water and made a cup of tea, then sat and sipped it, looking at nothing.

There was a knock at his door, and he got up to open it. Barrceil and Fanward were there.

"Hello, we heard," Barrceil said. "May we come in?" Hondoll stepped back and waved them in.

He made more tea for them and they sat in his living room. "Is the King mad at you too?" Hondoll finally asked.

"No, he likes us," Barrceil said. "He asked me to join his staff, in fact. I was polite, but I've been in private practice a long time. I don't mind doing a favor for the King but I don't want to be on salary. I turned him down and he didn't insist. He offered Fanward a place on his staff, too."

"Did you take it?" Hondoll asked.

"I couldn't," Fanward said. "The other magicians objected, because I don't have a degree and I'm not a member of the Collegium."

"I'm sorry about that, Fanward," Hondoll said, snorting. "Sometimes the Collegium is a bunch of self-important clerks." They were all silent for a while. Finally Hondoll said, "The King's not going to be able to stop the Birth-Day, not with troops and not with the magicians he's got."

"Do you think something's going to happen, aside from a bunch of fighting?" Barrceil said.

Hondoll was silent for a long while, then said, "I want to tell you something and get your opinions. Offand wrote down some spells in his notebook, and he was conscientious about recording his results. I invoked those equations, exactly as written, and the commotic coefficients in my results were a little different. Not much, just the last few digits, but different."

"You did his math and got a different answer?" Barrceil said. "Have you considered maybe you were just wrong?"

"Or Offand was," Hondoll said. "I checked over everything a couple of times, and then I was rattled, so I gave it to three other magicians and had them check the math. I wasn't wrong, and as near as I can tell Offand wasn't wrong either. But we got different answers."

"You think something has changed since Offand's day?" Fanward asked.

"Well, of course, it was different because the Deluge hadn't happened when Offand did his work. He triggered the Sorcerer's Deluge and he was the first to die in it. But we have always thought the Deluge just released energies that were already there. This is different – this makes me think the Deluge changed some kind of basic constants, or changed a balance of forces … I don't know, I don't understand this yet."

He stood and began to pace, saying, "Something changed, anyway. I'm thinking that all through human history, people have been worshiping screwball gods, and none of those cults ever added up to anything. The gods never actually appeared, they were just stories. Do you think maybe that's changed? Do you think maybe now these crazy people actually can raise crazy gods that will really exist?"

"Do you think that?" Barrceil asked.

"I'm still in theory mode," Hondoll said, smiling. "But yes, I'm beginning to be afraid that's exactly what will happen on the Birth-Day."

Fanward idly looked over the piles of things Hondoll had put on the floor, then reached out and plucked up the moon necklace Hondoll had bought in the plaza in Dry Harbor. "Doctor Hondoll, where did you get this?" he asked, holding it up.

Hondoll explained. Fanward continued, "The booth where you bought this, was it draped in Carche colors or Panhegan colors?"

Hondoll pursed his lips to think. "As well as I remember, neither," he finally said. "It might have been red cloth, or something. I don't think I even noticed that the booths had different colors at the time. I know there were at least a few people left in Dry Harbor who weren't members of either cult. Why do you ask?"

"This is the demon Diana, enemy to Carche," Fanward said. "They don't talk about her much outside of temple, but no merchant would touch this who was a follower of Carche. The funny thing is, I know Diana is also an enemy of Panhegan so they wouldn't have it, either. The fellow who sold it to you must not have known what it was, or he would have been afraid to display it."

"I noticed people looking at you when you bought that necklace," Barrceil said. "Maybe that's why they came to the beach to find you. I forget, were you wearing it while we were digging out Offand's boat?"

"I had it in my pouch," Hondoll said. He looked at the necklace and said, "This thing is just pewter. It was never expensive or important. I just wanted it because it's old and I like things about the Moon. 'Diana,' you say? That sounds feminine, but this looks like a man's face."

"Sometimes they talked about the 'Man in the Moon,' but that's supposed to be just another incarnation of Diana," Fanward said. "Take my advice and never show that in public. Diana is hated violently."

"Well, I suppose all religions have to have devils or boogey-men or something," Hondoll said. "I don't why they'd pick a pre-Deluge image like that, though."

"May I borrow that?" Barrceil asked. "I can see some possibilities." Hondoll nodded without interest and resumed his pacing.

But Fanward would not give up. He said, "Doctor Hondoll, Doctor Barrceil, where did the Moon go after the Deluge? Was it destroyed?"

Hondoll said, "I have a vague idea it wasn't destroyed, but where it went, I have no idea," and looked at Barrceil, who shrugged. "If you go to the university," he continued, "I'm sure you'll meet a lot of scholars who know more about it than I do. I can't promise they'll agree with each other. Is it important?"

"The Moon left," Fanward said, "and then math with commotic numbers started working differently. The Moon was a pretty big thing. The old fishermen have stories about the tides we used to have. People in town don't know about those anymore."

"Tides?" Barrceil said.

"The water level in the harbor used to go up and down several feet, twice a day. That's what a 'tide' is – we don't have them any more. The gravity of the Moon used to lift the water up, several feet when it was on the same side of the Earth and less when it was on the other side. Sometimes there were harbors that would only be full during the high tide, so you couldn't anchor there." Fanward waved his hands, trying to explain. "In the fisherman stories, it's always something like the ocean god was in love with Diana the Moon goddess and was trying to reach up to her. But I know the harbor at Dry Harbor used to be wet, because all the old boats are there, so I think something physical happened. It just seems to me something that big would cause a change when it went away, maybe a change in the way math works."

Barrceil said, "There's a scholar at the university named Yuthan who teaches astrology. He might know. He lives out in the river district, and he might remember me – I took his course. I could introduce you."

"Barrceil, why would you take a course like astrology?" Hondoll said, turning back toward her. "That's pure bunk."

"It was an easy grade," Barrceil said. "We weren't all little miniature geniuses in college, you know." Hondoll flushed.

"Would you introduce me, Doctor Barrceil?" Fanward said tactfully. "I'd appreciate that." Barrceil smiled and nodded.

Hondoll said, "Seriously, Fanward? Astrology? You know, when magic became real people started to believe in all of the other superstitious nonsense they had, even though all the rest of it was still fake. The university is rotten with it to this day – along with the real scholars and magicians, they have astrologers and alchemists and diviners who look at chicken entrails and I don't know what all. The math department always thought they were stupid but we couldn't say anything because all those departments had a vote on our budget. But you don't need to go looking for silly stuff like that." He stopped a moment, then said, "Now that I think about it, they used to call that 'chasing moonbeams.' Huh!"

"This Yuthan is also an amateur astronomer," Barrceil said. "He found some old books and studied them. We never were able to get a department of Astronomy at the university."

"You're right," Hondoll said, puzzled. "We had other sciences, why not astronomy?"

"I think know the answer to that," Fanward said ruefully. "I'm sure it's because anybody with the mathematical skill to be an astronomer could make more money as a magician or an astrologer or something. Anyway, I want to know where the Moon went."

"Suit yourself," Hondoll said, shrugging. He

continued, "Birth-Day is about two months away now, and I feel like I've got to do something. I'm going to go back to Dry Harbor."

"The King isn't going to let you work with him or with the Army," Barrceil said. "I know he's going there himself. That fiasco at your lecture has him worried."

"I can avoid them," Hondoll said. "I took an oath to defend the kingdom and I'm going to do it with the King's blessing or without it." He looked at the two of them in turn. "I mean seriously, what else am I going to do? Teach? Make beer cold? I used to be a weapon in the hand of the King and now I need something that isn't trivial to do."

"What are you going to do, Doctor Hondoll?" Fanward asked. "If you use any of those big spells the King will know, and I think you don't want to directly oppose him."

"I don't. I don't have any ideas right now," Hondoll said. "I guess it has to be magic, because I don't really have anything else to use. But if that fails … I don't know. Magic has never failed me before."

"The King told me to watch out for you, Hondoll," Barrceil said. "I'm going to continue that. I'll go with you."

"I'm going to go talk to this Yuthan," Fanward said. "But I feel like I still owe both of you a debt. I'll rejoin you later and we can all go to Dry Harbor."

Twelve

"Yuthan doesn't like magic or magicians, so don't travel there in any magical way," Barrceil had warned Fanward. "Also, he lives out on the river so you'll have to get there by boat. Watch yourself – it's a pretty rough district. I sent a message by a friend, so he knows you're coming."

Fanward strolled from Hondoll's apartment down to the river bank. He passed a blacksmith pounding out horseshoes, and after courteously asking permission, magically heated his work piece to be softer. The blacksmith paid him a few coins, and Fanward smiled at being able to practice magic openly. At a tavern he earned a few more coins calming down a belligerent drunk and freezing water for ice. Passing a wealthy old man in pain from arthritis, he temporarily relieved the man's pain although he could not cure the disease, because no magician understood the cause of arthritis well enough. By the time he arrived at the river's edge, he had enough money to rent a wooden skiff to get to Yuthan's house. The late afternoon sun was nearing the horizon.

It was an additional pleasure for Fanward to pole the little boat through the swirls of river water, exercising a skill he had learned as a child. The district where Yuthan lived was in the shallow, slow estuary where the river Braidwater flowed out of the city and into the ocean. The houses were old, built after the Deluge over the river, in the days when it was unsafe to live on shore. Some were built on wooden pilings but others were founded on concrete pillars left over from the old days. The water splashed and sluiced through the various obstacles, and there were slicks and debris floating on the surface. Fanward lifted his oil lantern (not wanting to use a magical light) and propelled his skiff up to one building after another, puzzling out the location of Yuthan's house.

Candles and lamps flared in the windows around him, and suspicious faces peered out. A boat propelled by four paddlers started toward Fanward, bound on what seemed bad business, robbery or worse. He covered his lantern, and in the darkness spoke and gestured a spell that opened a portal underwater in the river. The river water swirled down through the portal into a location Fanward was able to visualize from his fishing days, far out on the ocean. The current that was created slewed the other boat around and pulled it away from him. When they were far enough distant, he closed the portal, reopened his lantern and resumed his search.

Presently, in the last light of sunset, he found the house he was seeking. It was a two-story wooden structure built on a concrete platform that had survived the Deluge. The platform was twelve feet or more about the current water line. He tied up his skiff to one of the uprights and called loudly, "Hello the house!"

A woman in an apron came out of a door, looked at him and said, "Come on up!" She pulled out a coiled rope ladder which was fastened it at the top and unrolled it for him. Fanward extinguished his lantern and clambered up, and the woman retrieved her ladder and rolled it back up. "I'm Corro, Yuthan's wife," she said. "You'll be Fanward? Come on in, we heard you were coming." She led him into the house to a room lined with books and lit with an oil lamp. Yuthan was sitting at a table eating his supper, and he waved with his mouth full indicating that Fanward should sit down. Corro set a plate of food before Fanward, and then sat down to resume her own meal.

Fanward had been expecting a gray-haired scholar, but Yuthan was a relatively young man with a neatly trimmed beard and wavy dark hair, and his wife, when he had a chance to see her by lamplight, was handsome as well. "So you're interested in astronomy?" Yuthan asked genially.

"Yes," Fanward said, "and I'm told you're the authority."

"It's really just a hobby for me, but you're only too right," Yuthan said, taking more food. "It's hard enough to get students willing to do the mathematics for astrology, and not one in dozens is interested enough to go out at night and go stargazing. It's a neglected art."

Fanward ate his food, which was good, and looked around at the books on the walls. "You

114

have a lot of old books," he said inanely.

"We're very fortunate as many books survived the Deluge as did," Yuthan said. "The Deluge destroyed a lot of buildings, and then there were fires and raging mobs who set more fires. But people back then had books in lots of places that happened to stay out of the weather. I've been able to get about fifteen old books on astronomy, which are still interesting even though a lot of them are about distant objects I will never have the instruments to see. I also have about ten books on astrology that I can still read."

"Most of the astrology books were on such cheap paper you can't open them now. They fall to dust," his wife added.

"Also the old astrology books I could get are worthless now," Yuthan said. "That's why I could afford to buy them on my salary! I just have them as curiosities. We modern astrologers, we're having to reinvent the whole science from scratch."

"Why is that?" Fanward asked.

"Because the Moon is gone, and the old astrology doesn't make sense without the influence of the Moon. You probably don't know what the Moon was," Yuthan said, stabbing the air with his fork to make his point.

Fanward smiled and looked down at his plate. "As it happens, I came here specifically to ask you about the Moon," he said. "I want to know where it went. I'm told you might know."

Yuthan stared at him, then applied himself to

his supper for a while. When he finally spoke, he said, "Judging from your accent, you don't sound like the kind of man who wants to know about the Moon."

"I was born poor, yes," Fanward said. "But my town had a library and I read books."

Yuthan said nothing until his meal was done. He helped his wife carry dishes to the sink, then said to Fanward, "Let me erect your chart. When were you born?"

"May 3 in the sixth year of King Walmon's reign," Fanward said. "But I really want to talk about astronomy, not astrology."

"The chart comes first," Yuthan said, putting a pad of paper on the table and taking out pencils and a compass. "Time of day?"

"I don't know."

Yuthan snorted, then worked at his chart for a while. He consulted a book of tables which was hand-written, apparently by himself. Finally he looked up. "You're a magician," he said flatly.

"Yes."

"But you were something else also," Yuthan said. "What?"

"A fisherman," Fanward said. "I hope being a magician won't prejudice you against me."

"Oh, everybody's got to make a living," Yuthan said, unexpectedly mild. "I really don't care much if you're a magician. But all this" – he waved his hands expansively – "our crumby civilization, can you imagine what we could have if we tried to build the way our ancestors did instead of trying to cheat with magic? We're brilliant at mathematics, far beyond what the ancients knew, and yet over eight hundred years, flush toilets have only been re-invented since I was a boy. We don't have a tenth of what they had in the old days. The difference is, all of our creativity goes into magic. When you were a fisherman, you procured fish for people. That's a good service. As a magician, all you do is change the relationships between other things, creating nothing." He continued in a similar vein for minutes. Eventually his rant petered out, and he spread his hands and asked, "What do you want to know about the Moon?"

"Where did it go?" Fanward asked.

"It's in orbit around the Sun."

"What does that mean?"

"The Earth goes around the Sun once a year. The Moon used to go around the Earth, but now it goes around the Sun instead."

"Can we see it?"

Yuthan stood and said, "By coincidence, for the next couple of days, you can. Come on outside. Did you bring a coat? No? I'll loan you one, it gets chilly sitting out there." He led the way out an opposite door to an open part of the concrete platform, bringing a chair with him. There was another chair already outside, along with an apparatus consisting of a long metal tube mounted on a tripod.

"I come out here because it's on the side away from the city lights. Better to see the stars.

This is a telescope," Yuthan said. "Ever seen one?" Fanward shook his head. "It makes distant things look bigger. I had a glassblower in town make me some clear cakes of glass, and I had to grind them myself to make lenses. This telescope is new, but the idea goes back well before the Deluge."

"I know a spell for making distant things appear closer," Fanward said.

"Yes, yes, I know about that spell. One of the magic professors at the university showed it to me, and acted very superior about it. Look, magic only works for the magician and is based on his understanding, right?"

"Yes, but … I can set it up so you can look, even though I have to invoke the spell myself," Fanward said.

"Save it. The important point is the word 'understand'. Your spell will only let you see what you're trying to look for, something you already understand. It won't show you anything you haven't seen before because your mind won't know what you wanted to see."

Fanward frowned. "I've used it to look at distant ships and the shoreline."

"Because that's what you expected to see," Yuthan said. "The telescope, it shows you what's there even if you don't understand it." Yuthan turned and pointed. "Look at that bright star near the horizon. That's Venus, the evening star tonight."

"I see it," Fanward said obediently.

"Now I'm going to focus the telescope," Yuthan said. He dragged his chair behind the telescope, pointed it and twisted the eyepiece. Finally he said, "Look in here. Twist this to make the picture sharp, but don't shake or move the tube."

Fanward did so, then said in wonder, "The crescent! That's the moon? It's so small."

"No, no, the crescent is Venus. Look up and little to the left of the crescent. See that dot? That's the Moon. It's actually not near Venus, the planet just happened to be in the same direction."

"I can't see any details," Fanward said. "It's only a dot."

"That's all you can see at this distance," Yuthan said. "You'll just have to take my word for it, that's the Moon. That's where it went. By the way, did you know 'month' was the period it took for the Moon to go around the Earth?"

"No," Fanward said with annoyance. "I didn't know that."

Yuthan said "Stay here a moment," and went inside to fetch a bottle of wine. He poured a glass for each of them, then settled into the other chair. "All right, magician," he said. "Talk to me. Why are you interested in the Moon?"

Fanward talked earnestly for a long while, explaining about the cults, Hondoll's magic, and his fears that the new gods might become real.

At the end, Yuthan leaned forward. "By chance, you came to the right person. You don't need astronomy," he said, "you need astrology. I told you we have to reinvent the science now that the Moon is far away. Fanward, before the Deluge the Moon affected everything. Women's menstrual cycles – did you know those are a month long? Moods, the night sky, sexual drive, a hundred things were tied to the cycles of the Moon. You know about the tides?"

Fanward nodded. "Did you think," Yuthan continued, "that there was something special about ocean water, that it was drawn to the Moon? All water was drawn to the Moon, Fanward. The blood in your veins, the rheum between your organs, the sap of plants, the rain and clouds, the wine you drink, the tears you shed. All, all under the sway of the Moon. The Moon was the regulator, the clock mechanism that ruled the entire Earth. That influence permeated all of astrology, all of science. And now it's gone."

"What does that mean?" Fanward whispered.

"It means that things that were held in check by the Moon are unchecked now. The big God, I suppose it doesn't affect Him. But all the little neurotic gods men invented, they would have been regulated and maybe suppressed by the Moon. Now they're not. Hondoll may be right. These Unborn Gods might really be born this time."

"What can we do?"

"I can't think of a single thing," Yuthan said, leaning back with his wine, "unless somehow you can bring the Moon back to Earth."

Thirteen

It took a few days for Hondoll and Barrceil to get ready to travel to Dry Harbor. For one thing, Hondoll needed some clothing that would be less conspicuous than his court finery, and had to get a tailor to make it. He was quite capable of forming clothing from fabric by magic, but the result would have reflected his own meager level of tailoring skill.

Also, they both had also agreed to disguise themselves without using magic, to avoid the peril of having a magical disguise dissolved. But that meant more time lost visiting a local theater company and making an appointment with their make-up specialist, to get a new look and learn how to apply it so that it would appear natural. Hondoll merely lightened his hair and eyebrows and learned to walk with a head-down gait. But Barrceil cheerfully decided to capitalize on her natural, sunny beauty and became a sultry, dark-eyed siren in provocative clothing. "Of course they'll notice me," she said lightly, to Hondoll's questioning look. "But they won't know it's me, and that's what's important. The Panhegan men won't dare look at me when their wives are around, and their wives will look at me and just sniff. I'll let the Carche men know they're not good enough to give me the higher spiritual experience I want from their orgies. This will be fun."

Finally, their preparation meant a long impassioned evening in a tavern arguing about the significance of the Moon. Fanward had finally coaxed Yuthan to meet the others. Yuthan got off to a bad start by eyeing Barrceil and saying "Barrceil? Is that you? You look different, you look good. Are you all magicked-up?" Barrceil smiled sweetly at him, said hello and returned to the sweet liqueur she was drinking instead of her usual beer.

"Scholar Yuthan," Hondoll said with exaggerated courtesy, "thank you for coming here this evening. Let me buy you a beer. But I can't see how an astrologer can help us here. I'm afraid Fanward has wasted your time."

"Doctor Hondoll," Fanward said, "hear him out, please."

"We have some important decisions to make here tonight," Hondoll said.

"Doctor Hondoll," Fanward repeated, leaning forward and with his voice low, "hear him out." Hondoll glanced at Fanward with his eyebrows high, then leaned back in his chair and nodded. Yuthan sighed, then began explaining again about the astrological and physical influences of the Moon that he knew, and the non-physical effects he suspected. Hondoll listened without comment, but his face grew more and more supercilious.

Finally Fanward finished for him by saying, "That's why both cults have demonized the

'Moon Goddess.' They know the Moon would be death to their gods. That is, I presume the priests know it. They don't say that to their people, of course."

"This sounds like," Hondoll said mildly, "more moonbeams."

Yuthan pushed his chair back, scowling. "All right," he said. "I've done my part. Let the 'Birth-Day' bring out crazy gods. What do I care?"

"Yuthan," Fanward said, "you aren't likely to join in with either cult, are you?"

"Damn right I won't."

"Then you'll be a target for whichever group wins, or maybe both of them. Please stay with us."

Yuthan looked rebellious, then sat back down at the table. Hondoll asked, "Look, I've never had to look this up. How big is the Moon?"

Long distances were measured in "kings-rides," defined as the distance the King could comfortably ride on his best horse in a day. The standard was re-set each time a new King ascended to the throne. King Leovar had been young and strong when he took the throne and had had an excellent horse, so the current kings-ride was somewhat longer than it had been in the days of his father. Yuthan pulled out a notebook and did some arithmetic, then finally said, "It's a sphere about forty-two kings-rides in diameter."

"That big!" Hondoll exclaimed. "No wonder they could walk on it in the old days! How far away is it now?"

Yuthan did more figuring. "About a quarter-million kings-rides, give or take. It's moving away from us now, also."

"There is a limit on the amount of magical force one magician can exert," Hondoll said. "Every magician has run into that limit, although no one has ever been able to quantify what the limit is or in what units it might be measured. But in any event, I'm sure I can't move an object that big, and I don't think anybody in the kingdom could do more than I can."

"Also you'd die in the attempt," Yuthan said gloomily. "You can't live in space."

"Why not?" Barrceil asked.

"It's vacuum," Yuthan said.

"What's that?"

"No air. You can't breathe, your blood boils and you die. Also there's radiation that will kill you quickly."

Hondoll put both hands palm down on the table and said, "I can surround myself with air using a charm that envelops my whole body. I don't happen to know the expression right offhand, but I've seen it in a journal. What is 'radiation'?"

"It's like the light from the Sun," Yuthan said, stumbling in his explanation. "Except you can't see it. I mean, you can't see it except for the part that you can see. That part's okay."

"And why doesn't the 'radiation' kill us whenever the Sun is shining on us?" Hondoll asked.

"The air stops the bad part," Yuthan said.

"Then wouldn't the air I would surround myself with stop the 'radiation'?"

"You wouldn't have a thick-enough cushion of air," Yuthan said with exasperation. After much discussion and hand-waving, they finally established that there are many colors of light, that people can only see some of them, and that 'radiation' consists of some colors that would be harmful if they were not stopped by the atmosphere.

Hondoll waved an apron-clad serving girl over and paid for another round of drinks. "All right," he said at last. "I believe I could define the set of all the colors I can see and then take the inverse of that set, which would be all the colors I can't see, and block them on that basis. But look, this is all to the side. I can't bring back the Moon. We're going to have to find another way."

Yuthan stood and said to Hondoll, "You know, in astrology we use mathematics to describe real things in the real world. You should try that some time." He stalked out. Hondoll waved negligently to him as he left.

"Several companies of soldiers left for Dry Harbor yesterday, with horses and equipment," Barrceil said. "The King is going to try to build walls and guard posts around the city to keep anybody from getting in."

"The cultists have magicians," Fanward said, "so they can get around barriers like that."

"They don't have magicians like Barrceil and me," Hondoll said. "And after we teach you a few techniques you won't have found in schoolbooks, you either. Barrceil, you're more familiar with Dry Harbor than I am. Is there an inn you're familiar with that we could go to, before the whole town fills up with cultists?"

"I can think of a couple," Barrceil said. "Is there any reason we shouldn't go right away? We can always reach back for anything we need."

"Fanward, do you need a disguise?" Hondoll asked.

"I don't see why. Everybody tells me I don't look like a magician now."

"Because people know you in Dry Harbor," Hondoll said.

"Oh, right. All right, I'll fix myself up with magic tonight and get something non-magical tomorrow. But Barrceil, dressed like that, nobody's going to think you belong with the two of us."

"I'm counting on that," she said, with a dazzling smile. "You're a gentleman and Hondoll's not interested in girls, but nobody else needs to know that. Give me a minute." She opened tiny portals to various places in Dry Harbor and looked through them, an activity which excited no interest in a tavern in the city of River's Lover. When she found a place to enter a tavern without being seen, she expanded the portal and stepped through. In a few minutes she came back, asked Hondoll for some money, stepped back through to Dry Harbor, then came back and invited them all through the portal.

Hondoll conscientiously left a tip on the table as they left.

Fourteen

They were almost too late to get any inn-room in Dry Harbor. The place Barrceil had chosen was called The Half Bridge, a wooden building that filled the left half of the arch under an old traffic overpass that had survived the Deluge. The bridge was still relatively sound although most of the road it had supported was crumbled and unusable. A street still ran under the open half of the bridge. The inn had one room left when Barrceil sweet-talked the landlord into letting them in. It was at the top of two flights of uneven wooden stairs, and the flaking concrete under-side of the old bridge was their ceiling.

Letting a room out to a woman who looked like Barrceil didn't faze the landlord, but when she showed up with two men he was evidently a little rattled. He said, "Three? In that room? I must charge extra for the room, for bedding and also for food." Barrceil paid over the money with a sly smile that left the landlord speechless. He called for a boy to carry the bedding, then led them up the dark staircase to the top, holding a candle before him.

At the top landing, he unlocked the door and presented the big iron skeleton key to Barrceil with a leer. He lit a candle inside, and the boy dumped the bedclothes on the floor. The others waited until the two had returned downstairs, then entered the room.

"Ah, I've seen worse," Fanward said. "It's cleaner than some I've had, and look, we get a window." The window had a hinged wooden shutter over it and, when open, was high enough to let them see the hills around the city. Barrceil found another candle to light from the first one.

There was a peephole in the door, which Barrceil plugged with a rag. "Let's look around," she said. "That nasty landlord's the kind who would put an extra sneaky peephole into the wall or something, and I guarantee he'd come use it tonight with me and the two of you in this chicken coop." The three of them searched the walls and floor inch by inch, and presently Fanward found an open knothole in the wall opposite the single bed.

"Here," he said, "I can handle this. The trick is to show him what he wants to see." Fanward spoke the spell and traced the diagram to create a small portal, which he positioned right in front of the knothole. "That looks into a room in a whorehouse here in town," he said. "The old man will see something that will take his mind off wanting to look at us."

"I take it you're familiar enough with that whorehouse to establish a portal?" Hondoll asked with wry smile.

"I used to deliver fish every week to that establishment," Fanward said with a straight face.

Hondoll said, "Look, I'll stay here tonight in case somebody looks in or knocks on the door.

Let's arrange the blankets so it looks like two other people are sleeping on the floor. Then you two can go home and sleep more comfortably."

"Hondoll, you're being a little more courteous to us than usual," Barrceil said.

Hondoll considered that a few moments and then said, "Yes, I suppose I am."

"Thank you for that," Barrceil said, and added, "We should go visit the common room tonight, though, before we leave. They'll be talk if we don't."

"Yes. I want to take some time to talk to people, see what they're thinking," Hondoll said.

Fanward nodded. "Me, too. I don't really understand what's in their heads. Having been in a cult myself doesn't seem to help me at all with understanding them now." He added, "Will you be all right, Miss Barrceil? I'm here to help if you need me."

"I'm a magician," she said. "Thank you for the offer, but no man has been able to discomfort me for years now."

The common room was bright with oil lamps. Two dozen men and a few women were there sitting at three long tables, along with the tavern's two serving girls, who shuttled back and forth carrying clay mugs of beer and glasses of wine.

At the table for Panhegan pilgrims, everyone wore gray and black, and the women were separated at one end. At the Carche table they wore green and yellow, and at the third table a mix of various colors. The people at the Panhegan table waved cheerfully and invited the newcomers to sit with them, and the Carche people did the same. After glancing at each other, Hondoll went to sit at the Panhegan table, Barrceil sat with some of the women at the Carche table and Fanward took a place with the locals.

"My name's Tann," the man next to Hondoll said. "By your clothes, I'm guessing you're not a pilgrim of Panhegan and not here for the great day, eh?"

"I'm Dharal Ashman," Hondoll said. "Actually, I'm in town on business. I'm representing a guild of weavers back in River's Lover and I have fine soft fabrics to sell."

"For a merchant," Tann said, "you appear to be dressed like a common workman."

Hondoll held his smile for an awkward moment, then finally said "If I dress in fine clothing everyone assumes my prices are too high. In these clothes, I get more sales."

"Perhaps, perhaps," the man said amiably. "The town is filling up with pilgrims, eh? You can sell to them."

"I have heard that when the Army is finished building their wall, they won't allow pilgrims to enter."

"That's no matter. Panhegan will not be denied," Tann said casually. "There are ways to get around that. But as far as selling fabrics, if they're not in the Panhegan colors of gray and black, you'll have difficulty. We'll be running the town from now until the Birth-Day."

"I have black and gray, also some green and yellow," Hondoll said.

"Don't say that, Dharal," Tann said in a low voice. "I'm a tolerant man, but others aren't as easy as I am. Those who are not with us are against us, so you must not think of selling to both sides."

"The Carche followers are sitting right there," Hondoll said. "There doesn't seem to be any animosity."

"Oh, they're welcome to sit near us," Tann said, raising his voice so the other table could hear him. "They'll all be dead soon enough anyway, we can afford to be nice to them now." At the Carche table, a couple of the men acknowledged his insult with a friendly wave of their beer mugs, and went back to animated, bright conversation with Barrceil.

Fanward talked to the local, nonaffiliated men at his table. No one there seemed cheerful.

"Now that you mention it," Hondoll said to Tann, just to make conversation, "what will happen to clothes after the Birth-Day? Will you all still wear black and gray in the new world?"

"Of course we will," said the man on the other side of him, jumping in. "If Panhegan wanted us to wear other colors, the priests would tell us and we could have them. After his mighty Birth, the world will follow Panhegan's edicts."

"By no means," said a woman at the end of

the table. She was dressed in a dowdy gray gown. "We wear funeral colors to mourn for those who will die. After the Birth, they'll all be dead and there will be no further need to mourn. When the great day comes, I'm going to get a red dress and shoes that are pinker than a baby's fanny."

"Who will you get those from?" Tann asked, as Hondoll looked from one to the other. "In paradise, no one's going to want to weave or sew or make shoes."

"No one will weave or sew," another man chimed in. "We will just have such things, out of the bounty Panhegan will provide."

The discussion ran on and on, spiraling up into ever more fanciful speculations. The Panhegan pilgrims drank only sparingly, but over at Barrceil's table, the Carche families had gotten happily liquored up on beer and were singing a loud song about all the things they would do after the Birth of Carche, each verse more coarse than the last. They waved their mugs and banged them on the table, while the children sang loudest of all. Barrceil sat silent, with a carefully neutral expression.

The Panhegan followers found their conversations drowned out, glared at the others and started singing a solemn hymn of their own. The noise became painful.

Presently all of the locals got up and left, and Hondoll, Barrceil and Fanward did as well. They met just outside the door, thankful to get away from the tumult. Barrceil turned to one man and said, "Are they going to fight in there?"

"Probably not," the man said. "I've seen this before. They just make a lot of noise, but I think they're saving themselves for the big fight on this 'Birth-Day.' I wish they'd get it over with."

"Why doesn't the landlord just throw them all out?" another man asked.

"Because business has never been better for him," the first man said. "Pilgrims are coming from every direction. If you've got a room, you were in luck."

Eventually, the three went back inside and climbed the stairs to their room. The singing and yelling was still clearly audible. Hondoll avoided using a magical light and lit an ordinary candle. He sat down with the Offand notebook, leafing through it. The others opened portals and quietly went back to their own quarters.

Presently he composed himself for sleep. He was awakened during the night when someone pushed the rag out of the door peephole, but he was too sleepy to find out who it was before they fled. He went back to sleep.

Fifteen

"In the last three days," Hondoll said glumly, "they've divided up the whole town. Carche gets the east side, Panhegan gets the west side, the plaza's neutral territory. That's a lot of cooperation for two cults that hate each other. And why the hell are the King's troops not doing anything about it?"

He looked around the plaza. He was sitting with Barrceil and Fanward at an outdoor café, watching the crowds go past, shopping at the various booths. Superficially, the plaza looked no different than it had two weeks ago, but the eyes of the passersby were wary and they looked left and right as they walked. There was a steady traffic in and out of the two cult temples. The other people in the plaza tended to avoid eye contact.

There was a pack of "Eagles" loafing in front of the Carche temple, teenage boys dressed in green and yellow and with distinctive close caps. They affected elaborate canes which were in fact clubs, leaning on them and twirling them jauntily. They laughed and called out insults to everyone who came close. Hondoll looked at them with distaste, then averted his eyes to avoid attracting notice.

There was also a company of horse-mounted soldiers, milling about in no order and gossiping with each other. They ignored the Eagles, and anything going on in the plaza.

Barrceil wore another fancy dress in dark red, Fanward was dressed in work clothes that suited him, and Hondoll wore workman's clothes in a way that marked them instantly as a costume. The old woman who ran the café came up to serve them tea and a late lunch.

"It must be good for you, old mother," Fanward remarked politely to her, "to be here in the middle plaza where both cults are. If you were on either the east side or the west side, I suppose you'd have to please the cult in charge."

She snorted. "You think that? Here in the middle, I'm privileged to give free drinks and food to the Carche punks when they want to invade my place, the Panhegan punks when they come around and those damn King's men act just like their own gang when they want to sit here. I'd be better off if I only had to get robbed by one side."

Fanward muttered sympathy while Hondoll paid her. When the old woman moved away, Barrceil said, "The cults cooperate on a lot of things, now that I think about it. They both picked the same day for 'Birth-Day,' they divided up the town, they both knew you had the Offand notebook."

"I've been talking to the Panhegan people," Fanward said. "Too many people know me on the Carche side. Anyway, they all think the gods whisper directly to the priests. The priests never explain anything, they just tell their followers what to do."

Hondoll looked around again. "Lots of people going in and out of both temples," he said. "I didn't think about it before, but now that I look, all of booths near the Carche temple have their colors, all the booths near Panhegan are gray and black, and everybody's who's independent is in the middle."

"It wasn't that way before," Barrceil said. "The cult boys made all the merchants sort themselves out."

"The King's men didn't do it to keep the peace?"

"The King's men are as useless as trash fish," Fanward said. "I've seen the King in town, the last couple of days. He rides around and gives orders, and I guess the Army and Civic Guard officers all say 'Yes, sir!' and then ignore him when he leaves. They're not enforcing any of the rules against anybody."

"Careful," Barrceil said softly. "Don't be obvious looking, but here come the Panhegan boys."

Hondoll looked sidelong across the plaza. From the direction of the Panhegan temple, another pack of teenage boys was approaching. They were "Exemplars of Panhegan," dressed in dark gray with black stripes down their trousers, pledged to chastity and virtue, and carrying their own sticks. There was one girl in their midest, riding in a buggy pulled by her protectors. She also wore gray, but it was a clingy gray dress with a tight bodice that showed her cleavage, and a short skirt. Her lips were painted bright red. She was gaily smiling and flirting with all of the men outside her group, while the boys watched each man's face for any interest in return.

One of the Eagles glanced at her and did not look away quickly enough.

The Exemplars exploded with self-righteous rage, and with shouts of "Dishonor!" and "Insolence!" they ran toward the Eagles, sticks waving. The Eagles lifted their canes at the ready. In an instant the middle of the plaza was a melee, while everyone nearby ran away. A few of the Panhegan boys hustled their girl, who was giggling with triumph, to safety at one side.

The King's men looked down from their horses but did not stir.

The two gangs flailed away with their sticks, their faces painted with blood, their expressions joyous. They hovered around the individual fights, darted in to strike blows and danced back. Bodies fell to the pavement on both sides.

Hondoll and Fanward rose to their feet but hesitated. Barrceil was not deterred. She stood upright and spoke a spell with ringing clarity, while tracing its morphisms with a hand before her. Man-high, wobbling circles of distortion and reflection formed in the middle of the fight. The fight was instantly visual chaos, every fighter seeing the others in a mix of mirror images and water-rippling refraction, impossible to understand. The fight stumbled to a halt for a moment.

But Barrceil was outside of the affected area and clearly visible. In an instant, two of the Exemplars ran toward her and clouted her head with sticks, knocking her to the ground. Both Hondoll and Fanward turned to defend her but in the noise and chaos, could not concentrate enough to work magic. They battled the others with their hands, and Barrceil crawled away.

Some of the Eagles saw her and came after her, and Barrceil struggled to her feet and ran, hindered by high-heeled shoes. She sprinted across the plaza and down the alley at the side of the temple of Panhegan, emerging into the streets of Dry Harbor.

Before the Sorcerer's Deluge, the town that became Dry Harbor had been a place of wide streets, tidy houses and expansive lawns. But over eight hundred years, it had been easier to build houses on the remaining slabs of smooth pavement, using scattered bricks and wood. It was easier to toss garbage onto a midden then to carry it away for disposal. It was easier to create trails through parks and across lawns than to follow the old streets. Away from the town center, Dry Harbor now was a place of narrow, wriggling alleys and slatternly shacks, with occasional intersections that held shops.

Barrceil ran down a street of hovels, her hair matted with blood. She shook her head to try to clear it but gasped from the pain. People turned incuriously to watch her pass as she dodged around horse-drawn wagons and dodged through crowds. Behind her, a mixed group of teenage boys in two uniforms ran together after her, sticks at the ready, hooting and yelling. The crowds melted back to let them pass.

There was no pattern to the survival of buildings from before the Deluge, because the destruction had not been entirely physical. Buildings that had been exploded into single bricks were right next to buildings that were untouched. The old buildings that happened to survive rose above the shabby new city here and there: single-family ranch houses, gas stations, fast-food places and others. Their occupants had originally been squatters, but over the centuries, many of the families had come to treat their old buildings as though they were baronial estates.

Barrceil ran past the remains of an old strip mall, with six of the original glass-fronted stores used as homes and the blown-apart ends encrusted now with tacked-on animal barns. A shaven-headed man appeared at the door of one of the barns and waved her in. She hesitated, then darted into the shadow of the interior and stood gasping.

"Hello, Barrceil," he said gently. "You're safe now. Go down here." He pulled aside a storage rack, which turned out to be hinged and mounted on silent rollers. Behind was an opening onto a flight of stairs going down. Barrceil stumbled down the stairs and the man gently pulled the rack behind him, then closed the door to bring sudden silence.

The stairs went down one flight to a basement, which had ground-level glass brick panels to let in the daylight. At the base of the stairs, Barrceil stood breathing heavily, stupid with pain. She peered at the man for a moment, then said, "Rendenen?"

"Yes, I am," he said.

"What are ... is this some Panhegan place?"

"No. There have been some changes. I'm not a follower of Panhegan any more. Neither cult will find you here. Come on, you're bleeding. Let's get you fixed up." Rendenen led her to a couch and brought her water to drink. With another basin of water and a rag, he began to carefully clean her wounds. Other people came into the room and stood silently while he worked.

Rendenen invoked healing spells over Barrceil, and her blood flow stopped and clotted. Presently her pain subsided and she was able to rest more easily. She closed her eyes and subsided on the couch.

After a while she said, "You're underground. You're some kind of ... you know, underground movement?"

Rendenen smiled. "Some kind, yes. We're not entirely underground. We still have those glass-blocks where the sun shines in. The people who live up top, they're with us. They know we're here but they won't tell."

"Won't the kids or the soldiers see those

glass blocks and know somebody's down here?"

"They won't see them. We use an image-cloaking spell, and some other tricks to keep us from being noticed."

"Are you against the King?" Barrceil asked.

"No. We're against the cults, and these new gods," Rendenen said.

"Who are you?"

"I think you know us," Rendenen said.

A woman came forward to stand by Rendenen. "Remember me, Barrceil? The last time I saw you, you were about to graduate from the gymnasium."

"Elder Carmania!" Barrceil said. "From church at home! This is …?"

"The Church of the Blessed Sun, in Dry Harbor," Carmania said.

"I didn't know the church had gone underground."

"There are some things," Carmania said, smiling, "that we don't tell all of the congregation members. You caught us at the start of service. Can you stand up, dear? Come over here."

The basement was large, a shared space that had been common to all of the stores above. There were, Barrceil could see as she walked with her head held carefully upright to avoid pain, three dozen or more church members standing between the upright posts. They lined up near the glass-block windows, and Barrceil was led to a place in the line.

"The Sun is going down, and will shine a blessing on us through the windows," Carmania said.

"It's all wavy and distorted through that glass," Barrceil said tactlessly.

"But still the Sun, with a blessing of light for us," Carmania said serenely. "Now that you mention it, that's interesting. Wavy and distorted, but still the Sun. I should preach a sermon on that! But in any case, you need more than the rest of us right now, so you stand right here. A little over to the side ... yes, right there."

Led by another officiant, all the people sang together some of the old hymns Barrceil remembered from her childhood, but extremely softly so that the sound would not be audible outside the building. They sang "O Sun That Drives Out Darkness" and "This Mighty Sun-Filled Day" and "The Light, Our Hope."

The sun set in the west, early because of the autumn season, and the glass brick windows gradually filled with light, which shone on the faces of the people. Immediately in front of Barrceil, there happened to be a chink in the mortar around the glass brick. Carmania pointed as a tiny dot of bright, clear sunlight appeared on her clothes and slowly crept up to her face. "Only one person a day can get the special blessing, down here in this basement," Carmania said. "Today, we want you to have it."

Barrceil was crying as the bright dot slid up over her body.

Presently the sun set, and the service was over. Black-out curtains were hung over the glass brick and oil lamps lighted as they prepared an evening meal. Rendenen went up the stairs and returned with Hondoll and Fanward, who rushed forward to embrace Barrceil, very gingerly because her head still hurt.

"They're taking care of me – I'm okay. Are you all right?" Barrceil asked.

"We had to use lots of visible magic to defend ourselves, and fight a lot to follow you. Everybody knows we're magicians now," Hondoll said. "I don't think we can go back to that inn room, or appear in public at all. But what is all this, and Rendenen, why are you …?"

"Food first," Rendenden said. "Eat with us."

Sixteen

At the end of the meal, the various church members began to slip out to go home, one and two at a time to avoid attracting attention. "Since the Deluge, the Church of the Blessed Sun has had to hide occasionally, sometimes for years at a time," Carmania said to Barrceil. "We've been through this. In the years when we're accepted again and we come back out in the daylight, we don't talk about it much. The Panhegan and Carche people think they've run us out of town. Let them continue to think that."

Eventually the lamp-lit basement was almost empty. The people who slept there went off to their pallets, and several sword-carrying fighters and two magicians (both acquaintances of Barrceil's from school) kept guard watch. Hondoll and the others were left alone at their table.

"So, Rendenen. You're a sun worshiper now?" Hondoll said, sharply and without obvious sympathy.

"No, just claiming sanctuary," Rendenen said. "I'm ... I don't know what I have left, anymore. I had to fake my own death to get away from Panhegan. I happened to find the Blessed Sun church here while I was working for Panhegan, because I can see better through their magical cloaking than others, but I never told anybody else about it. When I had to get out I came here, and they took me in. Since then, I've improved their ability to hide a little."

"You had to fake your own death?" Barrceil said.

"Nobody resigns any more, at least not at the level I was at," Rendenen said. "There have been killings. You haven't heard about them because they've been at night, and covered up. Both cults have killed members of the other, and of course they go after any Sun or Ocean worshipers they can still find. I took one of the dead bodies and made it look like me long enough for it to get buried, then came here to hide. I've been here about a week."

"Thank you for finding me," Barrceil said. "That mob would have beaten me to death, I think."

"I left Carche behind. I left Panhegan behind. I left Hondoll behind. I can't afford to leave anybody else behind," Rendenen said with a rueful smile.

"Why did you leave the Panhegan cult?" Hondoll asked bluntly.

"I've learned some things, I know some things," Rendenen said. "Things they don't want anybody to know. For one, I think I know why both cults wanted the Offand notebook, and why you were led to find it."

"I've read that notebook through and through, and I haven't been able to see anything the cults would be interested in," Hondoll said.

"Not in the notebook, directly. There were some hints there that led me back to my old textbooks." Rendenen opened a pack and pulled out a well-thumbed textbook titled *Offand on Functors of Commotic Sets*.

Fanward reached out to touch it gently. "I've heard of this, never read it," he said. "I couldn't get it through the library."

"It's one of the advanced but standard texts," Hondoll said. "Rendenen and I were in the same class when we studied this. I've still got my copy at home."

"I kept my copy, too," said Barrceil. "But what brings you to this book, Rendenen?"

"The 'Wrong Theorem'," Rendenen said.

When Fanward looked questioningly at the others, Barrceil said, "It's kind of famous. It's one of the early theorems in the book, but it's wrong. I mean, the theorem is obviously okay because it's the basis of a whole lot of other stuff that we use every day. But Offand screwed up the proof, and nobody's ever been able to write a correct proof for it. It's one of the things students try to do every year. Sooner or later somebody will get famous proving it correctly."

"Offand mentioned that theorem in his notebook," Rendenen said. "You saw that, Hondoll? So I went back to the proof, and went through it line by line. I got the same result everybody gets. You work through it very carefully, and it reduces to '1=0.' I tried to prove it using a different path, and then another proof starting from a different place. I always got the same result. That theorem is based on a contradiction."

"And yet the theorem works, so there really can't be any contradiction," Hondoll said. "I guess Offand just knew intuitively it was true. Some fine day, somebody smarter than you, me or Offand will figure out the real proof, without the error."

Rendenen looked at him. "Hondoll," he said, "forgive me, but I was able to catch Barrceil running away because I happened to be watching you remotely, while you were sitting in the plaza. That's rude, I know, but I was. I saw that riot begin."

"Why were you doing that?"

"Because I still love you, and wanted to look at you," Rendenen said simply. "Yes, yes, relax. My personal problem doesn't put you under any obligation. I mention it because it's stupid of me to keep thinking of you that way, but I do it anyway. Will you accept, just for a moment, that people form pointless emotional connections?"

"Where are you going with this?" Hondoll asked.

"Contradictions don't exist in mathematics, right? All true math resolves without exceptions. Contradictions don't exist in the natural laws, physics and chemistry and all that, right? Animals don't have contradictions, nothing that is natural does. Okay so far? Now one more thing. People do have contradictions. We're full of them. We say things we don't mean, we believe things we don't actually believe and deny things we do believe, we're full of stupidity and error."

"All right," Hondoll said cautiously.

"People are part of the natural world. We live here," Rendenen said.

"I'm not following."

"Contradictions actually are a part of nature because *we* have them and *we* are part of nature," Rendenen said, leaning forward intensely. "Magical mathematics is the one field of math that is tied intimately to the mathematician and won't work without him or her. The mathematician has contradictions because all humans do. So here it is: magical math incorporates contradiction. It works, we use it every day, but it is based on contradiction just the same. The 'Wrong Theorem' actually *is* wrong, except that it works."

Barrceil and Fanward looked at each other. Barrceil said carefully, "That's a big jump."

"That would be the biggest jump in mathematics," Fanward said.

"Big enough that when Offand wrote something – we don't know what, hopefully never will know – when he wrote something that used that theorem, it touched off a reaction that destroyed civilization, flattened cities and blew the Moon away," Rendenen said. "That big."

Hondoll said, "What does that have to do with me getting a hunch about the Offand notebook?"

"Panhegan and Carche are not two separate gods. They're aspects of one single thing. Once I realized that, I could see the signs everywhere. That's why I couldn't stay – I'm sure the priests of both cults know that but they can't afford to let anyone say it. The two sides fight each other because the one thing is a thing of contradiction. It – that thing, the sum of both gods, whatever it is – wanted the notebook to be held by the cults to keep you from using it to hurt them, and at the same time each of the gods wanted you to find it so you would use it to hurt the other god. The one thing that is two gods is a thing of craziness and contradiction and irrationality, and the four of us at this table, among others, are responsible for it."

Rendenen was obviously making a dramatic pause, and eventually Fanward indulged him by asking, "How?"

"Because every time we use magic, the commotic vector – the second solution to the equation, the one we don't use and don't know where it goes – adds some instability to world. Offand touched off an explosion of stored-up instability when he released the Sorcerer's Deluge, which is what blew the Moon away. We – you and me and every magician – we've been replenishing that supply ever since. Every time we work a spell, that commotic vector makes the world more unstable."

"Other people are irrational and silly, and

always have been," Hondoll said gently. "Not just magicians."

"I don't have all the answers," Rendenen said. "There's something special about the contradictions that magic puts into the world, but I don't know exactly what. I do know, now, that these new gods are something we have because we made the world ready for them. They're opposed to all rationality, and they can destroy it. If they're born and get power over the world, that will be the end of magic and in fact, all mathematics and all rationality."

"I'm beginning to see," Hondoll said slowly. "Offand mentioned in the notebook that he had started seeing odd effects while he was developing magic. He thought there was an untapped pool of ... well, of something. Say, do the gods know they're part of the same entity?" Hondoll asked.

"It's hard to say, until they're born and can talk to us directly," Rendenen said. "But I get the impression, no. Actually, I think neither god is really very bright, which I suppose makes sense for a thing of irrationality."

"We need something that would be the enemy of irrationality," Fanward said suddenly. "Something that used to hold the irrationality in check but then stopped. Something we could use against the gods and each god could use against the other."

"Do you have some thing in mind, Fanward? Because I don't," Rendenen said in a gentle voice.

"I do," Fanward said. "Hondoll and Barrceil know it."

"It's not really a plan, we don't have any idea how to do it," Barrceil said. "But we have … I don't know, an idea. Not much more than that."

"Tell me," Rendenen said. "I'm in. I'm here to help. I'm asking for your help."

"Fanward, tell him about the Moon," Hondoll said.

"I know about the Moon," Rendenen said.

"You don't. We need to get the Moon back. Listen now."

Fanward explained, with Barrceil helping. He talked long into the night, and Rendenen's expression gradually changed from incredulity to surprise and then to thoughtfulness.

Eventually their talk ran out. Barrceil and Fanward opened portals to their own quarters and went back for the night. Hondoll also went back to his apartment, after watching Rendenen go to a pallet in the back of the basement.

Seventeen

Rendenen had the gift of flattery. At twilight the next day, he and Hondoll poled their way on a boat across the river to talk to Yuthan. Yuthan was sullen and obstinate at first, but within a few minutes of buttery conversation, Rendenen had him volubly showing off his astronomical prowess in a way Hondoll could never have brought out. Yuthan invited them back out on his porch to look at the Moon through his telescope.

"The telescope shows you the physical Moon," Yuthan said. "Astrology shows you the effects of the Moon. You'll need both."

"Thank you, Yuthan," Rendenen said in a noncommittal voice. "Can we see the Moon ourselves tonight?"

"Just barely," Yuthan said. "It's going around the back of the Sun, and in another few days it will be lost in the glare. But tonight, I think we can still catch it." He fiddled with the telescope, then invited the two to look.

Inevitably, both of them remarked on how small it looked. "If it can't be seen as it goes around the Sun, how are we ever going to find it?" Hondoll asked.

"I can give you coordinates," Yuthan said.

"No good. We can only transport ourselves to locations we can see or visualize."

"Yuthan," Rendenen said, "are you willing to

help us make a voyage to get the Moon back?"

"You mean go with you?" Yuthan asked. "In space. Not on your life. Or my life, I suppose I mean. I'm staying here."

"No, we'll make the trip. But listen, we can create a portal back to you across any distance as long as we can visualize your house here, or you. Suppose we go far up in the sky, then let you see what we are seeing. Could you look at the stars, or something, and point us in the right direction? Then we can go that direction for … I don't know, I'll have to ask you to explain how far, but in any case, then we can stop and ask directions again. After a few legs of the trip that way, we'll be able to see the Moon directly."

"I don't like the cults any more than you do," Yuthan said. "Yes, I can probably do that. Can you move the Moon back if you can see it?"

"We don't know," Hondoll said. "But Rendenen, I don't think you've heard this part. Going that high up means going into space. We could die from that."

They spent a few minutes explaining the concept of "space" to him, and eventually Rendenen asked, "Yuthan, what would we need to survive in space?"

"A supply of sweet air, a shell to keep in the air against the vacuum, protection against radiation, protection against both cold and heat," Yuthan said.

"What is 'radiation'?" Rendenen asked politely, and Yuthan went through the explanation again.

Rendenen and Hondoll lapsed into a rapid conversation of technical mathematics, to Yuthan's annoyance. They borrowed a pad of paper from him and scribbled equations, arguing and gesticulating, scratching out and re-writing. Yuthan watched them for a while, then said, "You two are lovers, aren't you?"

"No," Rendenen said, glancing at Hondoll. "Why do you ask? I mean, we're just talking mathematics right now."

"Sure you are. You argue like an old married couple," Yuthan said airily. "Carry on." They went back to their argument.

After half an hour, Rendenen straightened up and began speaking and diagramming a spell. A black sphere a little higher than a man began to form in the air over the river, at the edge of Yuthan's porch. It was wobbling and gassy at first, then firmed up to a solid.

"You had a spell for that?" Yuthan asked incredulously.

"It's made of several spells put together," Rendenen said. "The spherical barrier is called The Rolling Redoubt, the air inside comes from the Charm of Untiring Nourishment, the black lining is called Lightlessness and it should keep out 'radiation' even if I don't exactly know what that is. I can move the whole assembly with a spell called Reins."

Hondoll looked at it dubiously. "How would a person get in?" he asked.

Rendenen spoke again, and the sphere split into two halves along a vertical equator. The two halves yawned wide. "We just sit on the inner surface?" Hondoll asked.

"I suppose the good Yuthan can loan you us some chairs. They'll probably fit," Rendenen said.

"Oh, never mind. We'll need a clear window, so we can see the Moon," Hondoll said.

"Won't that let in the 'radiation?'" Rendenen asked.

"You won't need color to see the Moon," Yuthan pointed out. "Could you let in only one color and keep all the others out? That would keep out any harmful radiation."

"Um, maybe. Help me out here. Show me a light of one color," Rendenen said. Yuthan went in his house and talked to his wife, then came back with a candle lantern with a green glass shade and put it on the table. Rendenen looked at it, wrote on the pad of paper for a moment, then spoke a spell. The sphere changed to a transparent green color. After more adjustments by Rendenen, the surface smoothed out and the sphere looked like smooth green glass. They could see through it to the small lights of houses on the other side of the river.

"All right, let's try it," Hondoll said. "Yuthan, how high up do we have to go to be in 'space?'"

"Five or six kings-rides if you go straight up," Yuthan said.

"That'll take a few hours," Hondoll said.

"No," Rendenen said. "I can move this as fast as I want, I suppose. There's no way to find out except to find out. Let's give it a try."

"Just me," Hondoll said quickly. "You stay on the ground."

"It should be me," Rendenen said. "I made this, I know how to control it." The two looked at each other.

"Oh, you both want to play 'after you, dear sir!'" Yuthan said. "Both of you want to take the risk away from the other, am I right? Look, should we find someone else to go?"

"No," Hondoll said slowly, "a magician on the ground couldn't control this once it gets too high to see."

"We both go," Rendenen said firmly. He moved to the edge of the porch, split the sphere again and stepped decisively into the half-shell. Hondoll got in next to him. "Yuthan," Rendenen said, "if this works, we'll probably just ride this thing home. Would you bring our boat back to where we rented it?"

"Sure, sure," Yuthan said. He looked at the sphere and said, "Listen, you two take care, all right?"

"We will," Hondoll said. "This thing isn't really big enough for three, but once we get up there we'll open a portal back to you and let you look, anyway. Thanks for all your help. We'll be back. Confusion to these stupid gods!"

Yuthan nodded. The two halves of the sphere

closed. It was motionless for a minute, then silently rose up a few yards, went left, went right, settled downward. After another minute, it rose smoothly and silently up into the night sky and vanished.

*   *   *

In monochromatic green, Hondoll and Rendenen could see the lights of River's Lover below them, and the stars above. Rendenen guided them straight up at a speed neither of them had ever attempted before. Their green bubble was filled with the whoosh of air around it.

When they were high enough that the sound of air faded away, the lights of the city were invisible below them as well. "You'd never know anyone lived down there," Hondoll said wonderingly. "I always assumed humans made more of a mark on the world than that."

"It was brighter back in the old days, when they had electricity," Rendenen said. "Oil lamps and candles are pretty dim."

The stars were a green glory above them, thousands upon thousands. After a quarter of an hour, they rose out of the night into the sunshine. Rendenen slowed and stopped the sphere's movement. The interior of the sphere remained comfortable. Even limited just to green light, the sun was dazzling and Hondoll created a black rectangle outside of it to shade their eyes. They could see the horizon of Earth as a visible curve under the thin fuzzy rind of the atmosphere. They stared in wonder at the sight.

"Why have we never done something like this before?" Rendenen asked. "Before the Deluge, people traveled up this high. We've had the magic for years. Why don't we?"

"They came up here on big flaming rockets," Hondoll said, his voice small with awe. "I guess we just never thought that we could do it."

"We think pretty small these days," Rendenen said. "We do magic, but we don't use our math for anything more ambitious."

"Didn't they used to float around when they were up this high?"

"They were in orbit. We're in a fixed relationship back down to Yuthan's porch," Rendenen said. "I think we actually do weigh a little less, though."

"Do we?" Hondoll said, then added "Maybe so. I'm feeling a little giddy just from being here." After a few minutes of silence, he said, "I'm going to call Yuthan."

He visualized Yuthan's porch in his mind, and spoke a spell to open a portal back to it. Yuthan was still sitting there. His face was hard to see in darkness. "Hello, Yuthan. We made it into space," Hondoll said. "We're not ready to go get the Moon yet, but if we were, would you be able to tell us which direction to go?"

"Let me look," Yuthan said. He peered through the circular portal and said, "There are so many stars, and they're all green. The Moon's still in the Ecliptic plane, so we'll need one of the Zodiac constellations. Turn the view to your right. A little more. Okay, hold that a minute."

After a long pause, Yuthan said, "I think I know which way the portal is facing, now. We would do this in stages, right? I don't have to point you in exactly the right direction the first time?"

"Yes," Hondoll said. "Once you get us started, we can make corrections."

"Okay, I think I can figure it out," Yuthan said. "Let me see the ground."

"You need that to plot a course to the Moon?"

"No, I just want to look at it. Face the portal toward the part of Earth that has sunlight. I can't see anything on the dark ground." After a while Yuthan sighed and said, "Thank you. That's glorious. I'm still not going up in that thing."

"Thanks for your help. We'll be back to talk in a day or two." Hondoll closed the portal.

It was not yet the middle of the night in River's Lover, and the sphere presently rotated back into the shadow of the Earth. The stars leaped into greater prominence, and the sphere was filled with green light.

Hondoll looked at Rendenen. "I didn't see what was important about that reference in the notebook back to the Wrong Theorem," he said quietly. "You did. I also didn't figure out the significance of the Moon – Yuthan did that, and

Fanward saw what it meant. It looks like I'm not the smartest man in the room anymore."

Rendenen looked back at him. "That's a pretty big admission, for you," he said. "I don't think I've ever heard you say that before."

"I suppose I wouldn't say it if I weren't forced into it," Hondoll said. "Anyway, what I'm trying to say is that I need to love somebody I can look up to. I never really had that with you before. Now I do."

Rendenen snorted. "Hondoll," he said, "I loved you before, I still love you and I want your love in return. It must be your big brown eyes because it sure isn't your conversation. For pity's sake, you're going to have to do better than that if you want me back. You know I'm an excellent mathematician and you also know I can't add up a column of figures and get the same answer twice running, because arithmetic skill is sort of a different compartment in the mind. If you think I'm going to open myself up to a relationship that can go emotionally sour the first time I forget to carry the 2, you're crazier than Panhegan or Carche. If you want to say 'I love you,' try again from a different angle. A very different angle."

After a long time, Hondoll said, "I never said I was good at this."

"You never have been. Me, either. I suppose we belong together, because neither one of us is going to do any better."

"I could say that, and mean it," Hondoll said.

Rendenen, who was only marginally the

taller of the two, looked down at Hondoll and said, smiling, "You're cute when you're being sincere. Look at the stars with me, look at the Earth. It's beautiful up here, and we're going to have to go back down and be part of a really ugly fight. Talk to me when it's over."

"Do you think we'll be killed?"

"Not really," Rendenen said. "But we are going to be different people when this is over. Look, the Moon tamps down supernatural stuff, right?"

"That's what we're counting on."

"Offand invented commotic numbers and magic only a year or two before the Moon got blown away. Before that, mathematicians didn't have those things. Once we bring the Moon back, if we can, the commotic solution to magical equations starts losing potency. Don't you think the other solutions, the useful magic ones, are going to weaken the same way? Magic is going to be over."

"What happens to us?" Hondoll asked.

"I suppose we'll have to get jobs," Rendenen said lightly. "Hard to imagine, right? That's what I mean. We'll be different people. I'm not going going to believe you if you say "love" until you say it to the man I'm going to wind up being."

They reached across to hold hands, and presently Rendenen brought the sphere back down through the atmosphere and over the land to the city.

Eighteen

The next person to seek shelter in the Blessed Sun basement was the King.

Fanward brought him in, through a portal which he immediately closed. King Leovar collapsed on a chair, gasping and wild-eyed, his bloodied sword still in his hand. Carmania was there. She and Fanward both knew better than to get close to a man in his condition. They stood back, made vague soothing noises and waited for him to regain his control.

Carmania looked at Fanward and said, "Are they going to follow him here? Do we need to evacuate?"

"Give me some credit," Fanward said sourly. "I pulled him out of a battle in Blacksmith's Square and took him through two portals that go to places I know but no other magician is likely to be familiar with, before I brought him here. Nobody can trace him. What did you want me to do? He would have been killed if I'd left him there."

"What happened to the guards who are supposed to protect him?"

"No idea. He was getting attacked by Carche people on one side and Panhegan on the other. They left off attacking each other to go after him. He's just lucky I happened to see him. Look, he's hurt. Barrceil knows more about healing spells than I do. Is she here?"

"She's out getting food for us," Carmania said. "But we've got a woman here who knows about non-magic healing. Let her try." Carmania went through the dim basement and returned with a woman carrying a bag of medical supplies, who knelt down beside the King and talked to him calmly while she mopped a trickle of blood from his face with a cloth.

"Your Majesty, what…?" Fanward began, and the woman waved him back. "Talk later," she said. "Let me work."

The battle in Dry Harbor had come to the street outside the shelter. The screaming and clash of weapons was loud enough that the sound came through the glass block windows. The shelter was crowded with refugees now. Families huddled together, silent and tense, their eyes wide in the gloom.

"Fanward," Carmania said, "we'll talk to the King later. We've got two magicians maintaining defenses here but more would be better. Can you help?"

"Oh, certainly," Fanward said. "I'll go talk to them."

Gradually the King lapsed into sleep, slumped in the chair. His nurse stayed on guard to keep him from being bothered.

After a while, Barrceil returned with the three men who had helped her buy food. While they were setting up a table to prepare the food, she went to search out Fanward.

"The King?" she said, tilting her head toward him.

"I rescued him," Fanward said. "I was here watching the battles through portals, and saw him get attacked. I'm glad you got back all right."

"I had to go far out into the country to find little towns I've been to before, but where the fighting hasn't spread. Fanward, what the hell is going on? Were all these people members of the cults before and we just didn't know it, or did they just get swept up now?"

The defenses of the basement were fortified as well as they had been able. They had magical cloaking to keep anyone from noticing them, and magical and physical barriers around the perimeter. Besides the magicians, a dozen armed men waited by the door to the stable upstairs. At a quiet request from the other end of the basement, Fanward went back to do some homely kitchen magic, fetching water and boiling it to make soup, since they could not build a fire.

When the soup was ready, the sun was just going down. They put up the black-out curtains and Fanward created dim magical lights to float near the ceiling. The King roused himself in time to accept a bowl of soup from Carmania. "I'm safe here?" he asked thickly.

"You're safe, your Highness," she said.

"Bless you." While he was spooning up soup, Fanward and Barrceil came to him and sat nearby. "Fanward, Barrceil ... what are you doing here?" the King asked. "Never mind, you can tell me later. It's good to see some familiar faces."

"Highness, I can work some healing spells that require you to be awake and participate. May I do that for you?" Barrceil asked.

"Food first," Leovar grunted. He was pale and shaky. The nurse had bandaged one arm, and his head was wrapped with a bandage that was soaking through. Leovar ate for a while, then said, "Fanward, you're the one who saved me? Thank you."

"We're on your side, your Majesty," Fanward said.

"I don't have a side any more," the King said morosely. He applied himself to the soup for a few more minutes, then said, "I had to send my family out to our country estate. Some of my own guards turned against me. The others were killed fighting the traitors. Benjaric is dead, killed by another general I trusted. The Army must have been riddled with cultists. I never knew. I've failed."

"The Army is fighting on the side of the cultists now," Barrceil said. "Some units on one side, some on the other. They've divided the town up, with Panhegan on the west side and Carche on the east. Unfortunately, we're just about on the dividing line here, so they're fighting right outside."

"We can hide here?" Leovar asked, and when she nodded, said "Imagine that. Fighting in the kingdom, and the King is asking if he can hide."

When he put down his food, Barrceil worked a series of healing spells on him. They helped but did not take full effect immediately. Finally the King said, "Thank you, Barrceil. Carmania, this ... refuge ... was prepared by the Church of the Blessed Sun?" She nodded. "I was raised in the Church of the Ocean Mother, myself," the King said.

"Some of their people are here, too," Carmania said with a smile. "We're not rivals, haven't been for years. We serve the same God, not these senseless new ones. Be at ease."

"While my kingdom is being destroyed," he said. "I'm losing track. What's the date today?"

"December 20," Fanward said.

"The Birth-Day is tomorrow? Is there anything we can do?" the King continued.

Barrceil and Fanward looked at each other. "Sire, do you know what the Moon was?" Barrceil asked.

"My tutor taught me about that when I was a boy," the King said. "A big round thing that used to be in the sky?"

Fanward said, "We think it had an effect, regulating ... well, regulating Nature, I suppose. We think if we bring it back, it will suppress these non-rational gods. Hondoll and this other fellow Rendenen are trying to do that."

"Have they started yet?" the King asked sharply, and when Fanward looked blank, the King said, "Get in touch with them. Get them here, if you can. Right now."

Barrceil was easily able to visualize Hondoll well enough to open a portal in front of him without knowing his location. They talked quietly for a moment, then she expanded the portal and he and Rendenen stepped through. They turned and bowed to the King, and Hondoll introduced Rendenen.

"Hello, Hondoll. The Moon?" the King said. "That's your contribution to the kingdom, is to bring back the Moon? You can't stop the fighting, you can't stop these so-called gods from being born, you can't do anything that's actually useful, but you can bring back a big rock in the sky? You have a way to keep it from falling to the ground and destroying us all? Hondoll, I thought I told you to stay out of this. You and your friend, both."

Hondoll flushed deeply, and Rendenen's face was dark. "I've been convinced, your Majesty," Hondoll said. "Bringing back the Moon is the answer."

"I forbid it."

The magicians glanced at each other, and there was a long silence. Finally Hondoll said, "Your Majesty, I'm sorry to be disobedient, but I can't accept that." He began a spell to open a portal and leave. Nothing happened.

Fanward's magic lights flickered out and died, and the basement was dark. After a long moment, someone lit a single candle.

All four magicians began chanting spells, all

different, and tracing their diagrams with their fingers. There was no response. Rendenen said, "Magic has stopped working. Here, at least."

Someone in the dark near the glass brick wall said, "Listen. The noise just stopped. I think they're not fighting out there."

King Leovar said, "Let's go take a look. Something is happening."

"Your Highness, your injuries ..."

"I'm all right," the King said. "We need to see." Carmania gathered a few of the armed guards by eye. She, the King, the four magicians and the guards stepped quietly up the stairs and out through the stable.

The street was deserted. Standing under the stars, they could hear thousands of voices on the west side of the city softly singing a hymn to Panhegan. Other thousands on the east side sang to Carche. No one was in the middle of the city.

Barrceil said, "I think the birth has begun."

They were all silent for a long time. Finally the King said, "This road leads out of the town to the north. We'd better take advantage of this lull to get everyone as far away as we can. When the sun comes up, things could get a lot worse in this town."

"I think you're right, Sire," Carmania said. "Can you walk that far?"

"Other people are worse off than I am."

"We'd better start right away." Carmania went back downstairs to lead the refugees up.

"I'll go with you, Sire," Fanward said. "The

magic might come back once we're far enough away from this town. Maybe I can be helpful."

Rendenen and Hondoll looked at each other. Rendenen said, "We're going to walk out, too, and hope we can get to someplace where we can use magic. But we need to go faster. Sorry to leave you all." They started off together, walking briskly.

Barrceil said, "I'll stay in town, Sire, but I'll hide. I want to know what's happening."

The King said, "I hope you'll be alive to tell us, later, Barrceil. Stay out of sight."

Nineteen

The road out of Dry Harbor connected to an old pre-Deluge highway heading north, sometimes smooth and sometimes cracked and tumbled. Hondoll and Rendenen walked miles through farm country and then started up into the hills, attempting a simple spell every so often to see if it worked. They walked until dawn was lightening the upper air, but their magic had not returned so far. Climbing up the hillside, even where the road was smooth, was exhausting.

"I've got to stop," Rendenen said. "My feet are blistered and I don't know what to do if I can't do healing magic."

"I won't argue," Hondoll muttered. Rendenen led the way to a broken slab of pavement the right height to sit on, and he and Hondoll wearily watched the sun rise. Both pulled off their boots and rubbed their feet. They were elevated enough to see the town behind them, still puddled in shadows. Lights were visible on the east side and west side, but nothing in the center.

The shadow of hills to the east of town shortened as the sun rose, and the morning lit the west side, then the center, then the east side of town.

As they watched, a ring of light flashed out from the town, spreading over the landscape, passing over the two men in an instant. They looked at each other.

Another ring formed and swelled outward from the town, but this was a ring on the ground. As they watched, the ground seemed to swell and lift in an expanding circle, accompanied by a profound groan from the earth. They could also hear the sound of hymns sung by the Carche crowds on the east, and by the Panhegan crowds on the west. They were too far away for natural sound to travel; the singing must have been carried along with the wave.

The ground wave rolled smoothly toward them. They felt themselves lifted up as the roadbed rose under them, then dropped back down as the wave passed on. "That was not real," Hondoll said. "Look at the ground. Nothing is cracked, the rocks didn't move. We experienced that, but the physical ground didn't."

Rendenen silently gestured back toward the town. The ground under it appeared to be convulsing, heaving and rippling like a body in excruciating pain. The buildings were lifted and dropped, although none toppled. The wind brought more hymns, mixed now with the sounds of screaming and panic. "The sound comes with the image," Rendenen said. "Whichever god is being born, we're hearing its birth cries."

The earth shook and squirmed, and the disturbance divided into two centers of ripples, one east of the town, one west. As they watched, they could see, even from miles away, two dark floods of fleeing people, panic-stricken cultists racing away from the town.

The ripples spread across the landscape and began leaving artifacts behind them. The ground wrinkled into folds, dimples and hillocks that began to form two images. The images were bas-reliefs formed from streets and pastures, farm fields, creeks and forests. They were miles across, impressed into the landscape: Carche the snake on the east, Panhegan the dragon on the west.

The images of the gods began to move, flowing without friction across the ground. They stretched and curled around the hysterical mobs of cultists, blocking them and forcing them back into the town.

Hondoll tried the spell to create little lights in the air, and this time his spell worked. "They're distracted," he said. "The magic's back. Let's get out of here."

"We can't go to River's Lover," Rendenen said. "That's the obvious next place for them to go."

"There's a little town called Goat Creek I once visited, about as far away as I ever got. If it hasn't changed much I should be able to still visualize it," Hondoll said. He tried to open a portal, but it wobbled and collapsed twice. Finally he succeeded, and expanded the portal enough for them to walk through it.

They looked back at Dry Harbor. There were arches of bright light forming between the bodies of the two gods, swelling like bubbles high into the morning air and then vanishing. They saw the ground crack under the town with a sound too deep to be thunder. Then the cracks instantly healed: obviously not physical, but enough to send the crowds into more despairing wails.

The two gods drew back. Their images in the earth shrank and broke apart into patches, and the patches shrank to nothing. Their images formed in the sky, vast, luminous and airy. The snake and the dragon floated above the town, writhing in the morning air.

The gods curled to look down at their quaking followers.

The two magicians went to their portal, glanced back once and stepped through. They vanished from the hillside, and the portal dwindled and collapsed behind them.

They stepped out of the air into a quiet, small town square. Goat Creek was not large enough to support a town magician, and the people in the square were not used to seeing magicians arrive. They stared, and some stepped back a little. Hondoll and Rendenen turned and bowed slightly to them, smiling with well-practiced professional courtesy. Hondoll immediately tried another little spell and confirmed that it worked. Rendenen said, "I'm going to try to get in touch with Yuthan. Would you see if you can get some food and drink? I don't know how long we'll be gone."

"All right." Hondoll walked across the

square to bargain with some shopkeepers, while Rendenen began to open a portal back to Yuthan's house in River's Lover. He established the portal without difficulty and found Yuthan sitting at his table.

"Yuthan, the Birth has happened," he said without preliminaries. "We need your help to get us to the Moon. Will you help us?"

"Of course," Yuthan said. "But how are you doing this? Magic has stopped being effective anywhere in the city, since last night."

"I don't know how this works any better than you do," Rendenen said. "I suppose it's that I can use magic because it still works here even though it doesn't work on your end. Anyway, no time to lose. I'm going to re-create my vessel and when Hondoll comes back, we'll need you to point us the way to go."

"I'm ready," Yuthan said. Rendenen parked the portal to one side and began the series of spells to re-create his green-walled bubble vessel, to the consternation and wonderment of the rustics watching him. Hondoll returned with dried meat, cheese and wine in bottles, which he had paid for using ordinary money. The two of them entered the ship, and Rendenen brought the portal to Yuthan inboard as well. They waved to the onlookers, sealed the ship and floated up into the sky.

After a few minutes, they were high enough to see Dry Harbor again. The gods, white lively shapes larger than the town itself, were dancing around each other in the air. They were spitting fireballs at each other. Some of the fireballs apparently were also aimed at the ground, and smoke rose from burning buildings. The ship continued to rise.

When they were above the atmosphere, Rendenen asked for directions. Yuthan said, "Open up this portal for a moment." When Rendenen expanded the portal, Yuthan poked his head through and looked around at the green stars visible through the sphere. Eventually he pulled back and said, "Okay, you need to go in the direction of Leo for a few thousand king's-rides."

"Yuthan, I don't know where that is," Rendenen said with annoyed, exaggerated patience. Yuthan stuck his arm through the portal and pointed with a finger. Rendenen smoothly brought the ship around to that bearing and they soared away from Earth.

"Thank you," Rendenen said. "How long will this trip be?"

"How fast are you going?" Yuthan asked.

"No idea."

"Then I can't tell you how long it will be."

After a while, Rendenen asked, "Yuthan, are we headed in the right direction?"

Yuthan peered through the portal, picking out Zodiac constellations, and said, "Yes, as far as I can tell. Anyway, it's close enough to keep going that way for the next couple of hours. I'm going to go take care of a few things, all right?"

"Good enough. We'll be in touch,"

Rendenen said, and closed the portal. He and Hondoll were silent for a while, watching the Earth shrink rapidly behind them. The light from the battling gods was reduced to a flickering spot on the coastline.

"It must be bad in Dry Harbor," Hondoll said.

"That patch is getting bigger," Rendenen said. "They're growing." He added, "I don't know how fast we're going, but I'm going to try to speed up." He modified his spell, and the Earth shrank a little faster. There was no visible change in the stars around them.

The bubble was not in a free path, but was still referenced to the ground in Goat Creek, so they had gravity. Without chairs, they tended to slide together into the bottom of the sphere, and then uncomfortably pull back from each other. Hondoll brought out his provisions, and they ate meat and cheese in silence, marveling at the stars around them. Hondoll opened one of his bottles of wine and drank from the neck, not having a glass. He hesitated a moment, then passed it to Rendenen, who glanced at him and then drank the same way.

"I can't see Earth any more. We must be far away. We're getting lighter," Hondoll remarked eventually. Rendenen responded by chanting and gesturing another spell, and they felt themselves pulled back down to the floor of the bubble, having normal gravity or at least simulating it. They slid together again, but did not try to move apart.

"What was that spell?" Hondoll asked. "I don't know that one."

"It attracts one thing to another," Rendenen said. "Here, I'll show you." He pulled out his notebook and jotted down the equations. "I assumed we'd use that to attract the Moon to ourselves."

"I have another spell, that makes things move on a vector I can set," Hondoll said. "I was going to use that."

"We'll do both," Rendenen said, "and there's some other magic I can think of. I have no idea if they'll work effectively. I'm still having trouble visualizing how big this Moon thing really is."

Hondoll was silent for a long time. Eventually he said, "People used to live on the Moon, before the Deluge."

Rendenen gave him a questioning look and said, "I thought there was just one man in the moon, like on your necklace. Or just the Moon goddess, or something."

"Those were just mythology. There was some kind of colony there."

"If space is vacuum, and the Moon is in space, doesn't that mean it's vacuum there too? They didn't have magic in those days – how did anybody breathe?"

"Machines, I guess," Hondoll said. "Anyway, they had special houses they could live in. They're probably still there." He looked at Rendenen. "Wouldn't it be great to live there, get away from all the insanity and irrationality on Earth? Once we bring the Moon back, we could sit outside and look at the Earth."

"We?" Rendenen smiled. "You're thinking we should shack up together?"

"Um, yes."

Rendenen looked down, then said, "Hondoll, I love you. I never stopped loving you. I'm more sorry than I can say for the pain I've caused you. But we can't think about anything else if these gods are tearing the whole world apart. Everybody else we love is down there. Let's concentrate on this."

"I don't actually think we have enough power to do this," Hondoll said.

"I don't think so, either," Rendenen said, "but if we fail … I mean, who can stand against the power of an actual god? We don't dare fail."

Hondoll said nothing, but clasped Rendenen's hand. Presently they kissed, and held each other, looking at the green stars.

Whatever speed they were traveling at, it took most of a day before they saw the Moon before them. Yuthan had re-directed them a few times. The Moon was a gray crescent ahead of them. When they first noticed it, it was the size of a small coin. Gradually it swelled until it filled half the sky.

"That's the Moon?" Rendenen said. He brought the ship to a halt and they regarded it. "It's ugly, just a bare rock, and look how big it is. What are all the pimples?"

"Craters, where other rocks have fallen on it," Hondoll said. "They used to write poetry about the Moon. I don't know why. It's horrible."

Rendenen sighed, then said, "Let's try. I assume if we get it moving back along the direction we just came, that will bring it to Earth."

Rendenen invoked spells. Hondoll invoked spells. They tried more spells, scribbled in their notebooks and showed them to each other, changed terms and coefficients both with purpose and with the randomness of despair. Yuthan returned and looked out from his portal but had nothing to contribute.

The Moon did not move, at least not enough to see.

"We really don't have the power," Hondoll said, and Rendenen looked at him with bleak eyes.

Yuthan said, "Look out in space where this portal is facing. Back toward Earth. Do you see something?"

"Moving lights," Hondoll said.

"Someone is coming," Rendenen said.

Twenty

The road out of Dry Harbor was empty. On the east and west sides, the refugees could hear hymns and chanting, and they saw the lights of bonfires and torches. But the center of town was dark, and the stars were visible overhead.

There was no reason to try to hide. They walked quietly, talking in murmurs, stepping along as well as they could. They could not go quickly, hampered with old people, two cripples, little children and mothers carrying babies. The King tried to inspire them with his martial bearing, but he was limping slightly from wounds that had not yet finished healing.

They had about a dozen effective warriors with swords, who walked at the perimeter. Fanward was with the King. None of his magic worked and he could contribute only his own strength to the defense, which was not inconsiderable. But there was nothing to defend against.

They passed through a small market square and some of the men went to take food from the abandoned booths. "Wait," the King said. "Let's be upright." He opened his pouch and pulled out coins, and said, "Leave money for what we take. Money might not be any good in the morning, but for now, we're still good people."

"And worshipers of the Blessed Sun,"

Carmania said pointedly. "The Sun commands honesty, and we will comply."

They pressed on, fortified now with vegetables, preserved meats and bread. Some of the children cried, and were fed as they walked.

After half an hour of walking without incident, they were close to the edge of town. Fanward moved to be near Carmania. "Elder Carmania," he said, "I was raised in the church, but I fell away to join up with Carche. Now I don't know what to think. Where is the Sun in all this? Why does He let …" Fanward waved at the east and west sides of the town, "… let all of this happen? If the Sun rules the world, why does He want us to go through this? Where is the Sun?"

"The Sun is shining on the other side of the world right now, because they need sunshine too," Carmania said lightly, then made an airy motion with her hands. "No, I'm not being facetious. The Sun rises every morning and blesses us all with the day. He's the source of all life and warmth, given freely to everyone. But for a lot of people, that's not enough. They can't be grateful for that. They want a god who does tricks. Well, now we're seeing what kind of god you get when you want tricks. They can do the trick of canceling magic, and they're not even born yet. I think by tomorrow we'll see lots more tricks they can do."

"But why does the Sun let them do those things to us?"

"He doesn't. *We* let them do it. I don't know

what's different now, that these mad gods are becoming real when they were always just mythology before. You probably know more than I do about that. But right now, our job is to protect our people from the gods' followers. That's where your duty lies."

"Yes." Fanward looked at his hands, and said, "I never was much good at fist fights."

"Fanward," Carmania said, looking at him, "we have people here who can't fight. If we get caught, we don't dare try to fight, we have to run away. That's what you're supposed to help with. Buy us some time to get the old people and kids away."

"I wish I had my magic," Fanward muttered.

The weaker members of the march faltered as the night wore on. Fanward wound up carrying a sleeping toddler on his shoulders. Presently they left the town and walked into the farm country to the north.

Just before dawn, on a stretch of farm road with a ditch and a windbreak of trees on one side, they heard voices and footsteps ahead of them. King Leovar peered ahead, then motioned toward the side of the road. "Everybody down," he hissed. "Behind the trees, down in the ditch. Quiet for your lives. Swordsmen, to me."

The road was empty by the time the approaching party arrived. They carried cult banners, but in the uncertain light it was not possible to tell which cult they were members of. They had men, women and children, perhaps a hundred in all, and appeared to be pilgrims arriving late for the Birth-Day. The King and his men watched them from the ditch, and the others hid and were silent.

The Sun rose. When the pilgrims were almost past, a ring of light flashed out from the town and swept over the road. Everyone looked up.

They felt the ground rise under them, as though there were an earthquake. The refugees scrambled out of the ditch and stood to confront the amazed marchers. People in both parties fell down when the ground subsided under them, although the trees were not affected. King Leovar arranged his little force for defense, and armed men came out of the other party to face them. They stopped warily, looking at each other, separated by a few yards.

They could hear hymns from the city now, and felt the ground quiver and shake. Among the cultists, a big man who appeared to be their captain came forward, flourished his sword and said, "Declare yourselves."

"Refugees, leaving the city in hope of finding peace," the King said. "We have no quarrel with you."

"Peace is what will flow from this city when Panhegan is born," the captain said. "Declare yourselves! Do you serve Panhegan or evil?"

"I am King Leovar," the King said, stepping forward. "Do you recognize me?"

"I suppose you are, but it doesn't matter any

more," the captain said. "Who do you serve? Answer quickly!"

The farmland around them was flickering and moving in the dawn light, the fields heaving like the surface of a thick soup coming to a boil. While the King and Panhegan captain glared at each other, the rest of both parties stared wide-eyed at the landscape. The ground under them rose and fell again as another wave swept them, toppling most on both sides. As before, the trees were not affected.

The ground rose up yet again, but this time it was a moving hill, not a wave. The land tumbled and rolled them back toward the center of town. Mothers clutched their babies to them, and the swordsmen scrambled desperately to avoid impaling themselves or their colleagues on their weapons.

The Panhegan group recovered themselves first. Their leader roared at them, standing heroically on the tilting ground with his legs wide, as though he were on the deck of a pitching ship. "Into the town!" he cried. "It's where the god commands us anyway! Go, get on your feet, we know our place to be. Go, go!" The group began running along the road into town, slipping and falling, the women and children chased by the swordsmen.

The hill reared up and the crest began to curl over, like a breaking wave. Then it stopped, frozen in place, an unclimbable barrier extending as far as they could see in both directions. The movement of the ground ceased for a moment, and the refugees helped each other up.

There was a light in the air above them. As they craned their necks and watched in wonder, the luminous, miles-wide figures of the dragon Panhegan and the snake Carche lashed and curled in the sky above them. They spat fireballs at each other, and some of the fireballs landed on the ground.

"Get away from the trees, or anything that can catch fire," the King said. They began to trudge back along the road the way they had come, returning to the town. They could hear screaming now from both east and west, but there was no place else to go.

Twenty-One

During the night, Barrceil walked the empty streets out of the center of town toward the west. The Panhegan cultists had taken over an empty lot two blocks on a side, which was overgrown and filled with rubble. By the simple expedient of recruiting a thousand willing hands to carry away old stones and bricks, and pull up weeds, they had made a plaza for their ceremonies. They had a platform at one side, flanked by fires on either end that cast a flickering light.

It was no trick to sneak up on them. Barrceil merely walked to the ceremonial plaza and stood in the shadow of a building on one side. No one noticed her. The crowd, led by sweating and gesturing priests in gray robes, swayed and chanted in the firelight. They sang hymns, shouted out call-and-responses, and stepped back and forth in a rhythmic that was not quite a dance. Some of them had fainted, and lay unattended in the middle of the crowd.

The priests apparently had no scruples about using magic for their own purposes. As Barrceil cautiously watched, the Archpriest gestured to a magician beside him. The magician created an image of the Archpriest four or five times his actual height, and adjusted his booming, magic-amplified voice so that it seemed to come from the mouth of the image.

The Archpriest walked back and forth across the platform, and his image moved behind him. He prayed for Panhegan to birth himself, he prayed for the destruction of Carche, he prayed for the protection of his people from Carche and from retribution for their own sins. He called down anathema on Diana the Moon Goddess. His prayers and pacing never stopped. The other priests capered and gestured in front of him, working the crowd into ever higher levels of intoxication.

Presently, Barrceil walked quietly away, went back through the middle of town and visited the Carche ceremonies. They were similar.

At dawn, with the ground heaving and tearing and the sounds of hymns giving way to screaming, she found herself back at the center market.

She stepped into a fabric merchant's empty booth and, with a grin, spent a few minutes posturing and preening in imitation of a vain woman shopping. She minced from one end to the other, holding up fabrics against her arm. Eventually she picked out a sumptuous white fabric, found scissors and cut a length she could drape into a robe. She took a minute to comb out her hair and arrange Hondoll's man-in-the-moon necklace on her bosom, and did not neglect to find a place for a pencil and her mathematician's notebook.

When she went back to the street, she stepped like a high-born lady and headed west, back to the Panhegan plaza. The street appeared to be rolling and pitching under her feet, but with a magician's trained discipline, she found she could walk steadily, merely by disbelieving in the movement. She kept herself calm and strictly upright as hysterical cultists ran past her.

They dodged around her and kept running away from the ceremony site. Barrceil had no magic, but was protected solely by her haughty demeanor. Her beauty, her clean white robe and her serene gaze parted the crowd racing around her.

The ground cracked open in front of her, exposing a chasm with red lava at the bottom. A hundred cultists tumbled in, wailing, and fell to their deaths. Barrceil waited patiently, her face unmoved. After a minute the walls of the chasm came back together with a boom, and she resumed her walk. The ground was unmarked afterward: the chasm was not real, but the deaths were. Barrceil entered the ceremony grounds.

The crowd and all but one priest had fled. The remaining priest was an old man, white-faced and gasping from shock, clutching his wooden staff for support. He stared incredulously at Barrceil as she approached him, pacing steadily and looking directly at him. Then they both looked up involuntarily: the gods had taken to the air and were white images whirling around each other above them, spewing fireballs.

"Call him down, your Panhegan god," Barrceil said to the priest. "The Goddess Diana requires him to speak to me." She gestured modestly to point to her necklace. The priest stared at her open-mouthed for a moment and seemed about to speak, but one of the fireballs landed on the opposite side of the ceremony site. The priest cried out incoherently and fled, his arms waving.

Barrceil looked around, moving slowly and calmly to impress anyone watching, although in fact the area around her seemed deserted. She found a little safe space in the entrance to a stone building. It was protected from overhead attack by a thick stone lintel, so she located a chair and sat peacefully, watching the overhead battle.

In college, Barrceil had studied the giant-image spell the Archpriest's magician had used, but had never had occasion to wield it herself since it seemed gaudy and in poor taste. Magic still did not work, but she pulled out her notebook and whiled away a couple of hours recalling the equations, writing and amending them in her notebook until she was confident she had the correct structure. Fireballs fell on the town, but since the ceremony area had been cleaned and had nothing to burn, none of the fires were close enough to concern her.

Presently the battle in the air seemed to be tapering off. Barrceil tucked her pencil and notebook away and walked calmly to the center of the ceremony area. She stood, relaxed and not looking up, and waited.

Panhegan the dragon swooped overhead,

then circled back and settled out of the sky in front of her. Close up, he looked like a drawing of a dragon rather than a real beast, rendered in white lines and with the city ruins sometimes visible through his body. He twisted his head sinuously and looked around at her. When he spoke, it was with a soft human voice. His dragon lips did not move.

"You are?" he asked.

"A priestess of the Goddess Diana," Barrceil said.

"Diana has no agency in my presence."

"You are wrong. You have suppressed magic, but I can still do magic because I wield the power of the Goddess," Barrceil said. "See this coin? I can put it through the back of my hand without injury, which no one could do without magic. Watch carefully, now. One, two, three." The coin appeared to pass through her hand and fell, tinkling on the pavement.

Panhegan's dragon head turned and he eyed Barrceil with first one eye, then the other. It was an animal gesture, suggesting an animal nature. His eyes were small and lizard-like, and did not give the impression of intelligence. "You want?" he asked.

"Diana wants to help you," Barrceil said. "The Goddess Diana prefers your rectitude and dignity to the ribald and licentious Carche, and She wishes to ensure your victory. If the Moon is returned to orbit the Earth, Carche will be irresistibly erased – it will be as if he never existed. Diana will be stronger then, but she assures you She will share rule with you. You will not be troubled by other gods then."

"I can kill Carche."

"Perhaps you can, but then the same forces that led to his birth will lead to his re-birth," Barrceil said. "You will have to fight him to the death again, and again, and again. You need an ally. Diana offers her aid."

"The Moon may hurt Me as well," Panhegan said.

"You need not fear. Who can stand against the power of Panhegan?" Barrceil said. "You are stronger than Carche and will not be harmed."

"Where is Diana?"

"She is near the Moon, as She must always be. You will find her there."

"I go." Panhegan flexed his dragon wings, but rose into the sky without flapping and in fact without sound at all. When he had become a bright spot high above, the snake Carche rose from the town after him.

Barrceil sighed loudly and wiped her forehead. She returned to her chair and sat heavily, breathing deeply for a few minutes. Finally she took out her notebook and attempted the image spell. This time, the spell worked: magic had returned with the departure of the gods.

She canceled the image, then opened a portal to the university library in River's Lover and vanished.

A few minutes later, she stepped out of another portal into the main plaza of Dry Harbor. There were a few people there, shocked and silent. They paid no attention to her. Barrceil found a table at the unattended café, searched for wine and biscuits for herself, and sat to study the illustrations in the book.

Twenty-Two

The dragon Panhegan lay along the dark side of the Moon, an image of glowing white lines that looked green through the wall of the bubble. It looked like a three-dimensional drawing of a dragon rather than a solid beast. It sprawled across most of the diameter of the Moon, not quite reaching the poles on either side. "That thing is a hundred king's-rides long," Hondoll said.

"So is Carche," Rendenen said. They had watched the two gods approaching through space from the Earth, growing at every moment. Now Carche the snake was also a white-line image, hugging the ground on the sunny side of the Moon, stretching across most of the surface.

"They can't be solid, they can't have any weight," Hondoll said. "Not if they're blown up to that size."

"They can still exert force, though. I just realized. You know why they're touching the ground on both sides? They're *pushing*," Rendenen said in wonder. "Look at their bodies, they're getting flattened out. You can see muscles. They're trying to push the Moon in opposite directions. What is going on here?"

"I think they have to be exerting some kind of super-physical god force," Hondoll said, "but they act like animals so their bodies act like they're pushing physically on the Moon. I can't tell what's real and what we're just seeing any more."

"Look back," Rendenen said. "Where they came from. We've got more company." He pointed "down" past their feet, where another white shape was rising up, and growing as it approached.

"Can't be a third god, can it?" Hondoll said, worried.

The Moon visibly trembled from the opposing forces on both sides. Cracks formed across the surface. The two gods squirmed and humped their bodies, the very picture of two vertebrate animals trying to force a rock to move.

The third glowing shape sailed up through the starry sky and revealed itself as Barrceil, in the image of the goddess Diana. The image had Barrceil's face and body: she was a little too stocky and short for the traditional rendering of Diana. She was dressed in hunting robes and carried a bow and quiver of arrows. A crescent moon was wrapped around her shoulders, even as she floated in front of the actual Moon.

Her image was about the same size as the diameter of the Moon, comparable to the dragon and snake. The image wore Hondoll's man-in-the-moon necklace.

Barrceil opened a little portal inside the ship and spoke through it in a normal voice. "Hi, boys," she said. "Hondoll, Rendenen, Yuthan. I'm on the ground. Now that the gods have left, magic works on Earth again. I think you shouldn't get too close to either god, though, or your magical ship might fail."

"We're all right so far," Hondoll said. "Nice picture. Is that another moon behind you there?"

"Thanks," she said lightly. "The Moon is part of me, and I am part of it. It goes with the outfit."

"What's going on?" Rendenen asked.

"I went to Panhegan as a priest of Diana and convinced him that if he brings the Moon back, it will wipe out Carche. Carche followed him up here to make sure he doesn't do that. Panhegan is trying to push the Moon toward Earth and Carche is pushing it away."

"How did you talk Panhegan into that?" Hondoll asked. "Won't the Moon destroy him, too?"

"He's *stupid*," Barrceil said. "They both are. Creatures of unreason and contradiction."

"But why did you do that?" Rendenen asked.

"Because I knew you weren't going to have enough force to move the Moon by yourselves," Barrceil said.

"What do you think we can do now?" Rendenen asked, but Hondoll eagerly jumped in.

"I see it1 It's a vector sum," he said. "Yuthan, can you point the way back to the Earth?" Yuthan reached through the portal and pointed with a finger. "Look, those two ignoramuses are both putting force on the Moon, in opposite directions, adding up to zero movement," Hondoll said. "If we apply our little bit of force at an angle, we'll be able to make use of their much larger force to move the Moon, but in the direction we want it to go. Barrceil, you're brilliant."

"Yes," she said.

"If the gods feel us tugging on the Moon, won't both of them get angry and go after us?" Rendenen asked.

"You're too small for them to see right now," Barrceil said. "They don't know you're here. I'll get in the direction we have to go and they'll think it's me applying the force. They're afraid of me. I can help out with your spells too – as the real me on the ground, not as Diana, I mean. I'm getting confused."

Hondoll and Rendenen consulted again with Yuthan, who helped them pick out the constellation of Libra to aim for. They calculated an angle from what they assumed were the forces of the two gods, and talked to Barrceil about it. Her image floated through the sky at a speed no physical object could match, then stopped relative to the Moon.

Both gods turned their heads to look at the image of Diana, but did not stop pushing.

All three magicians invoked their spells, Hondoll and Rendenen looking directly at the Moon and Barrceil looking at it through her portal. When they had finished invoking their spells, they waited for minutes. Finally Rendenen said "Again," and they repeated the process.

The two gods continued their mad, stubborn quest to push the Moon in opposing directions, but the god's small eyes followed Diana, who appeared to be gesturing as though she were drawing the Moon to herself.

After another pause, Rendenen said "Again."

The Moon began to move slowly in the direction Yuthan had indicated. Rendenen wanted to re-apply their spells but Hondoll touched the back of his hand and said, "The spells remain in force. Let's see what happens if we just let them work."

"The Moon is moving faster than we are, toward us," Rendenen said. "I'm going to adjust our own movement to keep us from crashing down onto it."

After half an hour, the two men finally sat back and relaxed. Barrceil moved her Diana image over to Panhegan to talk to him. The dragon turned its head and audibly hissed at her, although the sound could not be physical. After a while she sailed around the Moon and talked to the snake Carche, with much the same reaction.

The two gods were moving around the Moon now, changing their point of pressure to try to foil the other. As each god moved, the other repositioned itself to counter the change. "How can they do the calculation to meet any change, and still be dumb enough to want to move the Moon to Earth?" Rendenen asked.

"They're shrewd enough to solve nearly any problem, being gods," Barrceil said. "They have tremendous mental power along with every other kind. But they're not smart enough to choose *what* problem they should solve. They just react. 'Smart' and 'stupid' aren't opposites, they exist at the same time."

After an hour of movement, Earth was not in sight and the stars appeared unchanged. Hondoll asked, "How fast are we going?"

"Again, I don't know," Rendenen said.

Barrceil said, "Yuthan, are we on a path where the Moon will go back into its old orbit?"

"I don't know. I don't think so, not yet," Yuthan said. "I just told you the general direction to go. We'll have to adjust the movement when we get closer."

"Do you know the difference," Hondoll asked, suddenly anxious, "between a path that will take the Moon into orbit and a path that would leading to crashing into Earth? I'm thinking the orbit path has to be a very narrow window of position and speed."

"No," Yuthan said. "I never studied that."

"What happens if the Moon hits the Earth?"

"The end of the world," Yuthan said, "and this time nothing theological about it."

Rendenen said, "We've either got to figure out how to put the Moon in orbit or turn it away from the Earth entirely. Yuthan, didn't they used to have artificial satellites they put into orbit? How did they do that?"

"It was called 'orbital insertion'," Yuthan said.

"Do you know how to do it?"

"No. I have a book, but I never read it. Never saw any reason I'd need to know about it," Yuthan said slowly.

Hondoll said, "So we might be taking out the insane gods, or we might be destroying the Earth. Yuthan, get me that book." Yuthan's face vanished from the portal as he went back to his bookshelves.

Hondoll continued, "I've got to find out how fast we're going, and I need a system that's better than Yuthan pointing to describe directions. Rendenen, Barrceil, can you help me with that?" Yuthan returned and thrust an old text titled "Orbital Mechanics" through the portal. Hondoll took the book and said, "Yuthan, can you find out what the mass of the Moon is? I'm going to need that, I think."

"What are you going to do?" Barrceil asked.

"I'm going to read the book," Hondoll said.

"You're going to read a book on a subject you know nothing about and learn it in however many hours we have until we get near Earth?" she said.

"Yes. Quiet please, I have to concentrate." Hondoll lit a little light of magic over the book and opened it.

On the Moon, the gods squirmed and thrust their bodies against the dry, cratered rock. The Moon moved against the backdrop of stars.

Twenty-Three

The King, Fanward and all the refugees looked up as the gods rose into the sky. Their writhing white shapes, dragon and snake, soared up into the clear morning air, grew smaller and smaller, and vanished.

The screaming of the cultists, Panhegan on the west and Carche on the east, began to fade. Presently Dry Harbor was quiet. Fanward, on a hunch, attempted a small spell and then said quietly, "Your Majesty, magic has returned. I can probably open a portal to some safe place."

"No, wait," the King said. "Let's find out where the gods are going to. We don't want to put these people into a place that might be worse than here. See if anyone needs healing, will you? Thanks." Fanward tried to explain that he was not good at healing spells and the King brushed him off with weary exasperation. "Do what you can," the King said.

To the swordsmen, the King said, "Stay alert. We don't know what the situation is here. We should try to get everybody back to that basement shelter if it's still there."

Many of the refugees were standing with Carmania, eyes closed and faces tilted up to the east, receiving a blessing from the morning Sun. She was chanting a prayer of thanksgiving on their behalf, her arms spread and her hands open to the sunlight.

The King waited politely until her prayer was ended, then began to lead the group back toward the center of Dry Harbor. They walked slowly, tending their injured and infirm. The birds, who had apparently been frightened away, began to return and the morning filled with their chirping. One of the swordsmen tapped the King on his arm and pointed, and the group stopped. There was little gathering of men and women ahead, wearing Carche green and yellow. The King led the way forward, flanked by Fanward and two swordsmen.

One old man walked toward them. He seemed dazed, and spoke slowly. "Carche is gone," he said. "We are … we are awake, for the first time in … are you the King?"

"I am," Leovar said. "Has the madness passed?"

"I, I," the old man stuttered, and looked back at his group to catch their eyes. He continued, "It may be so, your Majesty. We are … we don't want to fight any more. Please don't fight us. Do you have water?"

"We have," the King said. He called Carmania to his side and said, "Let's help them, but keep them separate. The gods might return, and then they might turn suddenly crazy again." She nodded, and went to talk to the Carche group.

They continued on, and came to a crowd of hundreds of gray-clad Panhegan cultists. They were milling around uncertainly, or sitting on the ground. When they looked up at the Carche cultists, their eyes were empty of hate, and indeed empty of any emotion or response. One of them was wearing priest's robes and came forward.

"Are you leading this flock?" the King asked him.

The priest gave him a look of incomprehension. "No one leads," he said, mumbling. "No one speaks to us. We are alone, alone, alone. The gods have left us, and we have nothing of our own now."

"Do you intend to keep fighting?" the King demanded, but the old priest only looked at him blankly.

"Let's go to the central plaza," the King said to his men. "If there's anyone left who can talk to us, they'll be there."

When he led his group down the street, all of the cultists drifted in behind him, having no better direction to their lives. Other groups from both cults joined them, all morose and silent. When they arrived at the plaza, the march had grown to hundreds.

The two temples of Panhegan and Carche were still standing when they arrived, and appeared unharmed. A group of Carche cultists brightened up and one of them said, "There are emergency supplies in the temple, stored away for the Birth-Day. Come on!" This caused the Panhegan group to remember the same thing about their temple. Groups mixed from both cults went into both temples and brought out dried foods, jugs of clean water, blankets, medicine and other provisions. The people began to help each other, gray and green-yellow alike.

Fanward came back up to the King, who glanced at him and said, "Sorry I was short with you, Fanward." Fanward pointed across the plaza to one of the outdoor cafés. Barrceil sat there at a table, drinking wine and idly leafing through a book. Fanward, the King and a couple of swordsmen approached her.

She looked up, distracted, and her eyes seemed to take a moment to clear. "Hello, your Majesty," she said presently. "Sorry, I'm maintaining an image spell a long way away and it's hard to talk at the same time."

"Please, Doctor Barrceil, we need you to tell us what you know," Fanward said.

"All right, I can take down the Goddess Diana for a while," she said. With gestures and speech, she blanked out her image far out in space, then faced them and said, "Hondoll and Rendenen are leading the gods to bring back the Moon."

"What will happen then?" the King asked.

"If they do it right, the Moon will go into orbit and the gods will be weakened, maybe killed outright."

"And if they don't do it right?" the King continued.

"The Moon strikes the Earth, and we all

204

die."

"What do you think is going to happen?"

"I can't predict. Hondoll's trying to figure out the path that leads to orbit," she said.

"How is he doing that?" Fanward asked.

"He's reading an old book on the subject. We're trying to help him with some of the arithmetic."

The King winced. "And I suppose there isn't anything else any of us can do to affect this?" he said.

"I'm afraid not, sire," Barrceil said.

"Is there any place we can send people that will be safe if the Moon falls?"

"No, Sire," Barrceil said, and Fanward somberly nodded agreement.

The King was silent a long moment, visibly wrestling with his anger at the situation and his impotence to do anything about it. Finally he said, "If we disperse the people widely, some may have a better chance to survive. I can't think of anything more helpful I can do for the Kingdom. If the Moon doesn't fall, we can bring them back. Both of you, start opening portals to locations as far away as you can visualize, and let's get as many people scattered as are willing to go."

Barrceil looked down, and said reluctantly, "Your Majesty, I can't accept that order. Hondoll and Rendenen need my help now. I have to stand by them."

Fanward said, "Sire, if we tell the people

why we're opening portals, there will be panic. If we don't tell them, they'll want to know why they should go. Many people don't trust magical portals anyway."

The King's face clouded up and he touched his sword as though he were about to use it. Then abruptly he sagged with fatigue, and his hand fell away. "Stand down," he told the swordsmen. "Do what you can. Don't tell anybody about the Moon." He sat at another table in the abandoned café, and was silent and withdrawn.

Twenty-Four

"Yuthan, do you have a slide rule?" Hondoll asked. His face was tight with concentration, anxiety and frustration. Yuthan rummaged around and passed a slide rule through the portal. Hondoll glanced at it, grabbed it and broke it savagely across his knee. The gesture seemed to relieve some of his tension. "Sorry," he said. "Not the astrology toy, a real slide rule. Also, do you have a pad of paper? Quickly, please." Yuthan searched again, and delivered both items.

Rendenen said quietly, "Here's our current speed. I can calculate a course as a change in degrees relative to our current path, whenever you tell me what you need."

"How long until we're near Earth?"

"An hour and a quarter, if the gods continue to push as they are."

Hondoll grunted, still looking down at Yuthan's text book. He scribbled on the pad of paper, balancing it awkwardly on his knee, after working the slide rule.

Barrceil's Diana image had vanished, then re-appeared outside the green bubble. She swooped down and spoke to each god separately, and was again met with hissing. They continued to push stubbornly against the Moon.

Hondoll said, "What was the original orbit of the Moon, back before the Deluge?"

"I don't know," Rendenen said, and was wise enough to add, "I'll find out quickly." He opened a portal to the university library in River's Lover and stood up, awkward on the spherical floor of the bubble, to step through it. After twenty minutes he returned and silently handed a paper to Hondoll, who read it carefully and made notes before returning to flipping the pages of the book.

Finally Hondoll leaned back and handed his pad of paper to Rendenen. "You steer," he said. "Take that heading, and slow us down about twelve king's-rides per hour below our current speed. When we're the right distance from Earth, we'll have to figure out some way to get the gods to let go of the Moon. Once it's moving freely, it should go into its old orbit."

"Are you sure?" Rendenen asked.

"Of course not. Don't ask silly questions," Hondoll snapped.

"I can handle the gods," Barrceil said. "I can modify this image I'm projecting."

The minutes passed silently, with terrible slowness. They all searched ahead for the Earth, and after a long time found it, a blue dot the size of a pea. It grew slowly, while Hondoll invoked a spell to measure the distance with magical, mathematical precision. At last he said, "Now."

Barrceil's Diana image instantly morphed into a replica of the Carche snake. She moved the false Carche to approach Panhegan, and the dragon abandoned the Moon to chase the snake.

In an instant, Barrceil's image vanished and appeared on the other side of the Moon in the form of a dragon. The real Carche leapt away from the Moon to chase the dragon.

The two gods whirled around each other, their mouths working as they spat out fireballs which passed harmlessly through each other's bodies, but created fresh craters when they landed on the surface of the Moon. The Moon, sailing free of their influence, approached the Earth.

"Is the Moon going around the Earth?" Rendenen said. "I can't tell if the path has changed."

Yuthan spoke up through his portal. "It takes a month to go around the Earth, if it's in the right orbit," he said. "You won't see a visible change in the path."

"Is there something special about being in orbit, as opposed to the Moon just being near the Earth?" Rendenen asked.

"There is," Yuthan said, "but it's an astrological effect, not anything I suppose you'd accept. I'm not going to argue with you, but orbit is where the Moon is naturally supposed to be and where it will have the most effect. Whatever the Moon did for us, I think it's starting to do those things again."

Barrceil said, "I'm going to take down my image. They're not paying attention any more anyway."

"We're not going to be able to get them to push again," Hondoll said. "For good or ill, we can't move the Moon any more. Our part is over." He looked gray and weary, and his eyes were red. He let the text book and pad of paper slip off his knees and fall to the floor of the bubble. Rendenen dared to put an arm around his shoulder, and Hondoll slumped down, his head on Rendenen's shoulder.

The gods swooped down, and were between the Moon and the Earth.

Barrceil said suddenly, "Rendenen, I think some parts of the bubble are getting thin, or changing color or something."

Rendenen looked, and Hondoll lifted his head to look at the bubble wall also. A tiny hole formed in the wall ahead of them, and air began to escape with a whistle. Rendenen instantly began a spell to patch it, but while he was speaking and tracing the morphisms, another part of the bubble wall began to thin, and a second small hole opened.

"We've got to get out of here," Rendenen said. "Yuthan, step back from your portal, I'm going to cancel it. Barrceil, where are you?"

"The big plaza in Dry Harbor," she said.

Rendenen tried to open a portal to that location, but the ring-shaped opening in the air wavered and was unreliable. Hondoll sat up and tried also, with the same result. "I don't think we can get there," Rendenen said, his voice wavering.

"You don't have to. I'm keeping this portal open, remember?" Barrceil said. "Whatever's happening, magic still works on my end, at least right now."

"Of course," Rendenen said. "I'm not thinking. Get us out of here, will you? The bubble's starting to fall to Earth, too."

Barrceil expanded her portal and both men stepped through it. Hondoll prudently reached back to take his papers and Yuthan's textbook, and also grabbed the remaining food and wine. In a moment the bubble was empty.

Hondoll and Rendenen climbed out of the air in Dry Harbor. They nodded to Barrceil and Fanward. She pointed to the King, still sunk in gloom at another table and paying no attention to anything around him. They were courteously silent, and took chairs quietly. Hondoll shared out the provisions they had bought in Goat Creek, what seemed like a lifetime before.

Around the plaza, the people were sorting themselves into little groups, talking quietly. Hondoll saw a half dozen troopers from the Army meeting together. Their uniforms were a little different from each other – apparently they had been in different units. Now they seemed to be trying to re-form a disciplined unit.

Looking up in the sky, Fanward said, "I don't see the Moon. Do you know where I should be looking?"

Hondoll shook his head. "I don't remember

what part of Earth we were over when we left."

"Do you suppose we'll see it before it falls, if it does?"

"I think it's probably in orbit," Hondoll said tonelessly. "Anyway, it's too late to change anything now. It either orbits or falls."

Abruptly the sky flashed with light. When they looked up, they saw the sky filled with irregular, glowing white lines. The blue morning sky showed between them. Everyone in the plaza stood and stared up, uncomprehending and open-mouthed.

Rendenen said, "What the hell? Can we get Yuthan here?"

"Yuthan won't know what that is," Barrceil said. "Nobody's ever seen this before, I think. Some kind of net, like a fisherman's net? Is the world being netted up by the gods?"

"Those lines are images of the gods, the dragon and snake," Hondoll said. "Thousands, maybe millions of images in the sky, all jumbled together. Pick out one point and you can trace them."

As they watched, the network of lines began simplifying, and the blue interstices grew larger. "They're combining," Rendenen said. As they watched, the images began merging together, two copies into one and then the combined images merging again. The images seemed to pop like soap bubbles, and even as they vanished, the remaining images were slowly falling, like autumn leaves.

The images of snake and dragon were not just merging with their own kind, they were merging with each other, snake into dragon and dragon into snake. As the net of white pencil strokes settled through the air above them, Hondoll and the others could see the millions of outlines snap together into thousands, into hundreds, into a single, undescribable image that touched the pavement of the plaza.

The paving blocks rose up, formed into a pair of small eyes that regarded the people in the plaza with animal unintelligence, and then the paving blocks subsided and became flat once again.

The King was watching with astonishment, along with everyone else. The plaza was expectant with shocked silence … and then every person in town began to talk at once.

"Do we have any magic?" Hondoll asked the others, attempting a spell himself. All of the magicians began to invoke spells. Some of the spells worked, some didn't. "Tell me what works and what doesn't," Hondoll said, taking notes on his pad of paper.

After a few minutes, he said "Got it. Anything whose derivation includes the Wrong Theorem is useless now. Any other mathematical expression that doesn't depend on that, still works. I think some of them are not as effective as they were." They stopped trying out spells.

"That cuts out at least three-quarters of all magic," Rendenen said.

"So it does," Hondoll said, "but I'm telling you, that's the new rule."

"You can run through every spell you know, which is pretty much everything ever published, in your head and within two minutes, and sort them out according to which ones are derived from the Wrong Theorem and which aren't," Rendenen said. "Hondoll, you're still the smartest person in the room."

Hondoll looked at him with real worry in his eyes. "I don't want to show off, any more," he said. "You'll help me deal with that?"

Rendenen smiled, with genuine warmth. "I will, if you'll have me," he said.

The King came over. "It's going to be a new world," he said inanely.

Barrceil said, "Maybe better. Without magic, we'll have to work harder, but that might be good for us."

"With only a little magic," Hondoll said, "mathematicians won't be able to make a living doing magic."

"So they'll go back to writing on blackboards," the King said. "There's a lot of precedent, from back before the Deluge."

"Math is always more fun," Barrceil said, grinning, "when you can't do anything practical with it."

Twenty-Five

The people of Dry Harbor in particular, and of the entire Kingdom, spent that night and the next morning talking to their neighbors, with eyes that were bleak with embarrassment and shame. They worked together, patching up the wounded, burying the dead, cleaning up the debris.

The King and his former magicians all met at the old waterfront of Dry Harbor at sunrise. It was becoming the new waterfront. For the first time in eight centuries, the tide was coming in.

The water streaming into the old harbor bed from the ocean was filthy with debris, smelled bad and was foamy with dirt. But it rose smoothly, and lapped against what was left of the old concrete wharves left over from before the Sorcerer's Deluge.

Hondoll pointed out Offand's old sail boat. "We cleaned out the mud from inside it, remember? The hull is fiberglass and it's still good, so it should float. Look at it now, look quick." He and the others watched as the water lifted the old boat up. It floated at a tilt, but it floated.

"Your Majesty, may we have that boat?" Hondoll asked the King.

"*Now* you're asking for my permission?" the King said, but smiled. "Sure, I suppose it belongs to the Kingdom because it doesn't belong to anybody else, so I make you a gift of it. If you got a new boat, I think it would be a lot cleaner."

"We can't make portals anymore," Hondoll said, holding Rendenen's hand. "And Rendenen and I don't feel like trying to walk home from Dry Harbor a second time – we've *had* that experience, thank you very much. So we'll try to sail home."

Barrceil and Fanward both tried to speak at once. Finally Fanward said, "You'll need a sail. Also, that mast doesn't look too solid to me. Also, trust me that there are some things you'll need to learn about sailing, and I don't think there's any textbook here even if we could get you one back in the university library."

"We'll get a sail, we'll learn to use it. We've been cheating the world with magic all this time, but now we'll have to do things the one-step-at-a-time method," Hondoll said, and looked at Rendenen.

"We're going to do things one step at a time," he said again. "Take the path, not skip anything."

"All right," the King laughed. "I'm going back to my palace to see what I might still be the King of. I don't want to walk either, but being a practical man I'm going to find a horse. Barrceil, Fanward, will you ride back with me?"

"I suppose," Fanward said. "I get terrible chafing from riding a horse."

"I can heal that," Barrceil said. "That's one of the spells that still works."

"There is still magic that works," Hondoll said. "Not as much, maybe not as good, but there was magic before the Deluge and there will never be a time without magic, to the end of the world." He looked at Rendenen, then at each of the others in turn and said simply, "Magic."

Afterward

This book owes a lot to two books I love. The first one is a relatively new book, a popular work on mathematics by Eugenia Cheng called *How to Bake Pi* (2015, Basic Books). It's about a branch of mathematics called "category theory," explained with (yes, really) recipes and other homely kitchen references. Category theory is an attempt to organize all of the other branches of math into a framework that shows off their similarities. That is, category theory embraces the study of numbers, the study of shapes, the study of changes and all the other things mathematicians are interested in, and gives a sort of "alphabetical order" to the collection.

Now, I am not a mathematician, I'm just an irresponsible fantasy writer. I lifted a bunch of cool words (really, could any word be more magical than "morphism"?), and some interesting real ideas. There are also a number of interesting but quite wrong ideas of my own here, sparked by this book. But no one will learn anything about category theory by reading my book! For that, you want to read Dr. Cheng's book, which is easy to read and understand, and accessible to anyone. Dr. Cheng also has a bunch of interesting YouTube videos, on category theory and other topics.

Dr. Cheng, my humble thanks!

(Other math stuff: Rendenen's little speech about being a brilliant mathematician who can't add up a column of numbers and get the same answer twice, comes from an autobiographical note by Henri Poincaré. I also got a lot of interesting mathematical flavor from Eric Temple Bell's *Men of Mathematics* (1937). Now that I've mentioned Professor Bell, I should probably add a shout-out to that excellent science-fiction-writing guy John Taine, too.)

The other book I want to call out is Jack Vance's fantasy *The Dying Earth* (1950, many editions). Now all of you Jack Vance fans, settle down! Of course my book is not any kind of pre- or se-quel to Dying Earth, is not set in that world and has no direct relation to it at all. Also, I wouldn't care for the horse-laughs I'd earn if I tried to compare my writing to Vance's.

But those of you who love this book, do you remember when Turjan enters his apprenticeship to the wizard Pandelume and begins to learn ...

> ... a strange abstract lore that Pandelume termed "Mathematics."
> "Within this instrument," said Pandelume, "resides the Universe. Passive in itself and not of sorcery, it elucidates every problem, each phase of existence, all the secrets of time and space. Your spells and runes are built upon its power and codified according to a great underlying mosaic of

magic. The design of this mosaic we cannot surmise; our knowledge is didactic, empirical, arbitrary. Phandaal glimpsed the pattern and so was able to formulate many of the spells which bear his name. I have endeavored through the ages to break the clouded glass, but so far my research has failed. He who discovers the pattern will know all of sorcery and be a man powerful beyond comprehension."

So Turjan applied himself to the study and learned many of the simpler routines.

"I find herein a wonderful beauty," he told Pandelume. "This is no science, this is art, where equations fall away to elements like resolving chords, and where always prevails a symmetry either explicit or multiplex, but always of a crystalline serenity."

(My hero's name Hondoll rhymes with Phandaal. Kicker, or overkill?)

And of course I've taken inspiration (or swiped elements, whichever way you want to say it) from other stories in this book, such as the vanished Moon. I borrowed the idea of the god created by the worship of his people (*T'sais*) and the idea of two rival gods and their cultists (*Ulan Dhor*). I stole the name "The Charm of Untiring Nourishment." The lynx-eyed reader will no doubt find other references: I've been reading and re-reading this book since I was a boy.

To the late Jack Vance, my humble thanks also!

I want to thank my wife Kathie for love, support and proof-reading, and my friends at the Indie City Writers' Workshop who critiqued many chapters of this book and improved them.

The swell cover illustration is stock art from iStock.com, done by a Thai artist named Tithi Luadthong, who goes by the name "Grandfailure." He's on a number of different stock-art sites and if you like beautiful SF and fantasy art, it's worth searching on his stuff even if you have no publishing ambitions.

You're welcome to visit me at *CharlesOtt.com*.